D1825538

JUNGLE

JUNGLE SERIES BOOK 1

JUNGLE

Alan Berkshire

4 Horsemen
Publications, Inc.

Jungle
Copyright © 2021 Alan Berkshire. All rights reserved.

4 Horsemen Publications, Inc.
1497 Main St. Suite 169
Dunedin, FL 34698
4horsemenpublications.com
info@4horsemenpublications.com

Cover by 4 Horsemen Publications, Inc.
Typesetting by Autumn Skye
Edited by Heather Teele

All rights to the work within are reserved to the author and publisher. No part of this publication may be reproduced, stored in a retrieval system, or transmitted in any form or by any means, electronic, mechanical, photocopying, recording, scanning, or otherwise, except as permitted under Section 107 or 108 of the 1976 International Copyright Act, without prior written permission except in brief quotations embodied in critical articles and reviews. Please contact either the Publisher or Author to gain permission.

This book is meant as a reference guide. All characters, organizations, and events portrayed in this novel are either products of the author's imagination or are used fictitiously. All brands, quotes, and cited work respectfully belong to the original rights holders and bear no affiliation to the authors or publisher.

Library of Congress Control Number: 2022932810

Paperback ISBN-13: 978-1-64450-567-0
Hardcover ISBN-13: 978-1-64450-615-8
Audiobook ISBN-13: 978-1-64450-566-3
Ebook ISBN-13: 978-1-64450-565-6

For Nick and Maria Elena, two very important people...

Contents

One

End of November 2018
WELLINGHAM

Patience.

That's all it took. Patience and the willingness to remain perfectly still for hours on end, in all weathers: sun, rain, or snow. The problem was they were as nervous as I was, hanging back in the shadows, waiting, watching, just like me. Staying in one place too long, especially this place, was dangerous. Once it was a family park: green hills, woods, a boating lake, a safe place. Now, monsters lurked in the trees, lots of monsters. But there was food here—much needed food— and that outweighed the danger...

Maybe...

I *needed* fresh meat; it was a need, a craving. Over the last few days, it damn well filled my every waking moment, growing stronger not day by day but hour by hour. Corned beef, hotdogs, beef stew in cans, potted chicken—I guess these arguably could be called meat, protein, sustenance. But they aren't. They're not succulent, roasted, tear-it-off-the-bone-with-your-teeth meat, grease-dribbling-down-your-chin meat, getting-stuck-between-your-teeth-meat...

Christ! I'm obsessing!

Sundown was only a couple of hours away; if my potential dinner was going to make a move on the corn I left piled tantalisingly in the open, it would have to be soon. I could almost sense them in the shadows of the burnt undergrowth just beyond the rusted chain-link fence, noses twitching, scenting the air, long ears flicking, casting about like omnidirectional microphones picking up even the slightest sound.

Satisfied it was safe, but still cautious, the rabbit broke cover, only a few hops before it scrambled under the loose fencing, then remained motionless, eyes darting this way and that.

It was a beauty, maybe two and a half feet long, plump and sleek, but still wary. I needed it to come farther into the clearing, make the shot easier, surer. Sighting through the NcStar scope, I flicked down the safety on the L96 air rifle, my left forefinger curling around the trigger. I caught my breath as a second rabbit appeared behind the first, then a third, slipping under the fence, flanks twitching, ready to bolt at the first sign of danger but edging toward the corn, the enticing mound of corn so very close.

Clamping down on my elation, I considered the problem I now faced. My AGM L96 was a bolt action air rifle. I knew I was well practised, but was I fast enough to bag these rabbits before they scattered?

The corn proved too much of a temptation. The second rabbit passed the first, hopping eagerly toward the glistening golden pile. Carefully, I shifted my aim, trying not to think too much, allowing reflex to take over. I had ten to fourteen pounds of much needed meat in my sights, compliments of the Dust that made all things grow, like these beauties over three times their normal size. I didn't want to blow it.

Through the lens, I watched as they gorged themselves on the corn, eating fast, conscious of their exposure. I squeezed the trigger. The first rabbit flopped, the top of its head gone. My hands flew; working the bolt like lightning, I fired. The second rabbit was knocked off its feet as it turned to run. Half rising, I sighted the third rabbit dashing for the break in the fence. I pulled the trigger, and the fleeing rabbit somersaulted, skidding in the dirt, stone dead.

"Hah!" I punched the air triumphantly, knees popping as I got to my feet, long hours of remaining motionless taking their toll. "Not getting any younger, pal," I muttered ruefully.

Chambering another pellet, I clicked the rifle's safety on. I'd been here too long. Since the black Dust fell, rural

Southeast England was no longer a green and pleasant land; in fact, it was downright dangerous. If it wasn't sentient venomous vines, it was the Creeps—the monsters in the trees. Time to go.

Keeping a wary eye on the surrounding foliage, I hauled the two closest kills together, tying their back legs with a cord hanging from my belt pouch. The weight over my shoulder was pleasing. Just these two felt in excess of fifteen pounds. More than I had first thought...

The growl was low, menacing, a drawn-out rumbling behind me. Remaining motionless, my hand tightening on the rifle, I slowly cranked my head around. The dog crouched in the dirt thirty or so feet away, amber eyes glaring, strings of saliva hanging from its massive jaws, black lips drawn back over long, vicious teeth, ears flat to the huge skull. It was a monster. Beneath matted fur, heavy slabs of muscle rippled with appalling power, ready to burst out in bloody carnage at the slightest provocation.

Thirty feet... I didn't know if a single .25 pellet would be enough to drop the brute. I figured I would just have time for a second shot...

The rattling of the chain link fence made my blood run cold. There was a scrabbling in the dirt behind me to the left. Half afraid to look, I flicked my eyes around as a large Dobermann shook Dust from its black and brown hide. Dark eyes shone as it dropped its head between its powerful shoulders, snarling. Horrified, I watched as a third dog, another Dobermann, scrabbled through the rent in the fence to stand beside its bestial companion. Smaller, but nonetheless big in its own right, it yipped and pranced excitedly, tongue lolling from its wet mouth. Ebony eyes rolling, the dog looked at me then at the dead rabbit stretched out midway between us, scenting the blood on the air. I might have got the first dog with the rifle, but three?

No chance.

Slowly, making no sudden movements, I slipped the rifle from my left hand to my right, clicking off the safety. My left hand stole behind, fingers curling around the butt of a Glock 17 nestled in the small of my back.

I'm fucked.

If I turn and run, I'm fucked.

If the dogs attack all at once, I'm fucked.
If I use the Glock, I'm fucked.

I could probably kill all three dogs with the pistol, but the noise would be horrendous in the still late afternoon air that noise would bring the Creeps down on me as sure as shit. If that happened … I was fucked.

I was pissed about losing the rabbit, but it was a small price to pay not to be ripped apart by oversized, blood-crazed dogs. I slowly drew the Glock, letting it hang at my side, my thumb slipping the safety off as I took a small step backwards, then another, keeping it smooth and easy, my gaze averted so as not to antagonise the dogs. They were becoming agitated, especially the small one, taking jerky steps and yipping excitedly, then pulling back, jaws snapping, saliva flew.

"Shit…" I cursed under my breath as the other two dogs also started to get nervous, growling, red tongues lashing their drooling lips.

I took another step backwards, then another, creating more distance between us. Beyond the mesh fence, Denford Park loomed, falling into shadow as evening dropped her dusky cloak. Once a well-kept and manicured parkland enjoyed by happy families and dog walkers, the place was now a vast, overgrown jungle of grotesque trees, bitter bushes, and terse grass. It was as dense and treacherous as any African jungle or Amazon rainforest, continually growing, spreading out, choking the life out of tiny suburb of Wellingham at a terrifying rate, again, courtesy of the Dust that makes all things grow, like the rabbits over my shoulder and the canine monsters menacing me.

The smaller Dobermann was becoming frantic, snapping the air, making faux lunges at the bloodied rabbit; only the warning growls of the bigger mongrel dog held it in check. Harsh, sharp, barks echoed through the trees as the excited youngster began to yell, eager for fresh meat. My heart leapt into my mouth. Fighting the urge to run, I took three small steps farther away, my left hand aching as I gripped the pistol tightly.

It wasn't just about the snaking vines and twisted trees in the park, nor was it the rampant choking under-growth—it was the Creeps. There lay the true danger.

Carnivorous, fast, silent, they inhabited the dense woodlands like shadows, a cross between a lizard and an ape; at least, that's how I saw them. They weren't much bigger than chimpanzees, and like chimpanzees, they travelled in troops of anything between twenty and thirty in number. But that's where any similarity ended... I had no idea where these creatures came from, or what they were doing in the southern counties of England, but here they were, and they were vicious, savage, extremely proficient killers. If the barking dogs attracted them, it was all over.

My only hope was getting as far away from here as possible, try and head down Wellingham High Street, and get back to the Block and safety.

The smell of blood and guts was driving the smaller dog crazy. I had shot the rabbit in haste; it wasn't a clean kill, and the belly had been torn wide open. The young Dobermann rushed forward eagerly, barking excitedly. The huge mongrel exploded from the ground, streaking across the short distance to plow into the impatient pup. The excited barks turned into howls of pain and terror as the bigger dog snapped and bit ferociously at the stricken Dobermann, bearing it to the dirt, jaws tearing at its throat and sides, drawing blood. Howling pitifully, the dog tried to escape the savage attack as the mongrel caught it in his bloodied maw, lifting it and throwing it across the clearing. It rolled, crashed into the fencing, and lay there cowering.

Seeing its chance, the other Dobermann lunged for the rabbit, only to be confronted by a snarling, red-eyed apparition with blood dripping from its foaming jaws standing over its intended prize. The mongrel snapped at the dog's face as it frantically tried to veer away, its paws scrabbling on the loose dirt.

Seizing the moment, I backed away, keeping an eye on the squabbling dogs until I was far enough away to run. I crossed the dirty, cracked tarmac of Park Vista Road, seeking refuge behind a row of parked cars. My last vision was of the mongrel snatching up the rabbit and biting it clean in half in a shower of blood and guts, wolfing the bloodied meat down in huge gulps.

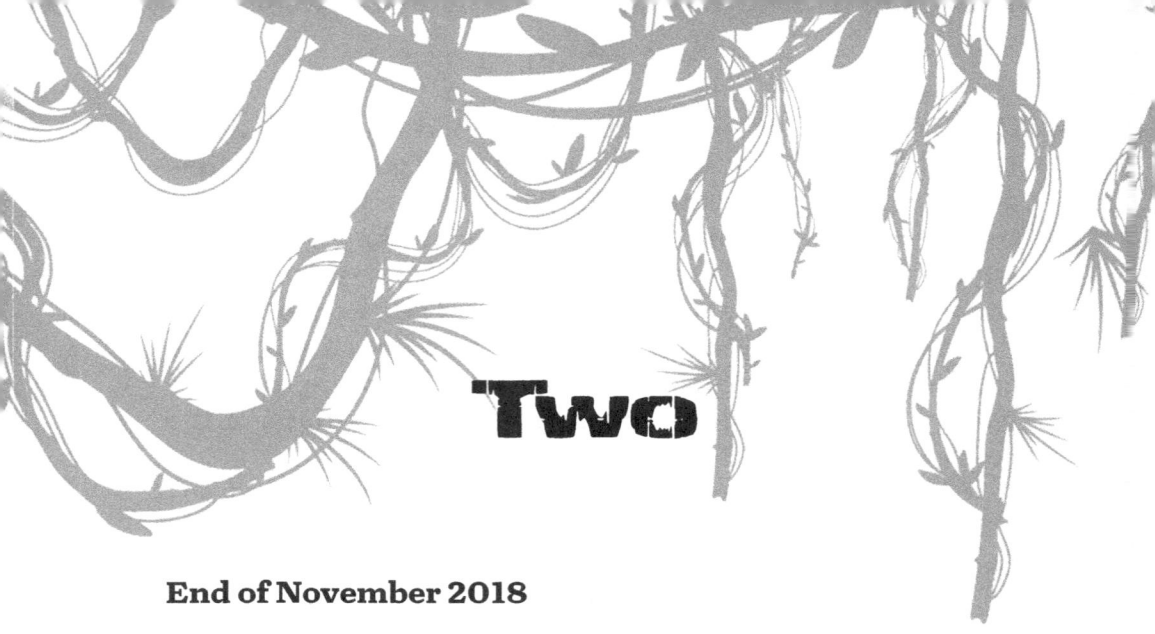

Two

End of November 2018

My bike wasn't far. Full night had not yet descended. Dusk hung just over the horizon like an impatient lover as I walked the deserted streets of Wellingham. Despite earlier events, I was safe enough. Predators were few and far between, and away from the park, I was able to use my guns if need be without fear of attracting the Creeps. I walked past silent, empty houses, windows like soulless black eyes surveying the once bustling neighbourhood, the streets now forlorn, cluttered with garbage and trash blown about by an indifferent wind.

Everything was grey in varying shades, a total absence of colour, no flowers, no bushes, and no green, just patches of charred ash, grass, vegetation, and trees. Someone had even gone so far as to smash all the flowerpots and window boxes, leaving nothing to grow, not a single blade of grass. The sterile desolation around me was depressing.

Jesus! Had it been nearly ten months? It felt like ten years since the Dust fell from the sky, a crazy mixed up emotional frightening time. It was still hard to take it all in...

It had been the beginning of March 2018. The weatherman promised a bright sunny, spring day. Talk about getting it wrong! Wellingham woke up to a thick precipitation of fine, black Dust that swirled and billowed like a living thing getting everywhere, covering everything, drifting like miniature black dunes in every corner, against every wall, every nook and cranny. It fell for over a week, stopping only briefly on the fourth day for about thirty minutes, then it continued to fall, heavier than ever, filling the streets, drowning the roads, engulfing cars...

I watched from my front door, the Dust swirling about me, cloying, as if I were somehow attracting it to me. It was impossible to stay on the doorstep for more than a few seconds. The black Dust filled my nose and throat, choking me. I was unable to see anything, hear anything. The Dust blinded me, dampened all sound. A quick check from the other windows of my first floor flat confirmed the Dust was falling on all sides. My mobile phone had no service, and the television was a disconcerting parody of the conditions outside, only white snow filling the screen instead of black. Fear began to creep in when the radio produced nothing but static, then I remembered my laptop. I should have known as I stared at the error message staring back at me from the screen: "No internet connection available."

"Shit..."

I was on my own.

The next few hours were a sort of blank. Weighing my options was easy; I didn't have any. At one point, my mouth and nose covered by a scarf, I went back to the front door. I opened it and was greeted by a cloud of billowing black; I took a few steps beyond the threshold, squinting against the Dust.

"Hello! Hello! Can anyone hear me? Is there anyone there? Hello!"

My shouts sounded hollow and flat. Seized by a sudden coughing fit, despite the scarf, I was forced back inside, slamming the door behind me. It was hopeless. No one could venture out into the Dust storm. Visibility was zero, effectively deaf, and you'd be lost within seconds.

The silence made it hard to sleep. I mean it was total, complete silence: no traffic noise, no activity in the street, not even a breath of wind to rattle the windows. I lay in my bed in a pitch-black room—despite the curtains being open—staring at an unseen ceiling. Finally, I got up and switched on the bedside lamp, fully aware of my sigh of relief.

I'd spent the day pacing my small flat, moving from room to room, compulsively checking my useless mobile. Come one o'clock in the afternoon, I got hungry and realised another problem: I didn't have any food in, just a few tins of baked beans and a half loaf of sliced bread. The cheese in the refrigerator was already growing its own plant life. Checking the taps, I was relieved to discover I still had water, the same with electricity. At least I still had the basic amenities—God knew for how long—I tried not to dwell on that. So, beans on toast it was. A cheerless dinner, especially considering I had intended to go out to Wetherspoons that evening for a burger and a beer.

From my bedroom window, I could see the Dust showed no indication of slowing, so as night drew on, according to my bedside clock, I went to bed. Four hours later, my bedside digital glared balefully at me in green, glowing numerical delight... Two forty-five a.m.

"Fuck..."

I didn't shout. I didn't even use my normal tone of voice, more a disbelieving whisper as I looked out the window the following morning, the black Dust continuing its silent deluge.

"What the hell is this?"

I had read somewhere that sand from the Sahara Desert had once been sucked into the stratosphere and deposited on some island off the English coast thousands of miles away. But black sand? And for nearly two days? I didn't think so. This wasn't that; this was something else. But what? I'd checked the Dust that had blown in the front door yesterday, fearing it wasn't Dust but ash. Visions of nuclear fallout lurked at the back of my mind. It was a relief to discover it was just dust, soft, powdery Dust.

I was at a loss. And I was starting to get really scared. I was stranded in my flat with food for maybe two more meals on a very limited menu. I could have beans on toast (again) or toast with beans... What can I say? I was a single man living alone... Smiling thinly at my own grim humour, I sat at the kitchen table, trying to think. I obviously wasn't the only one in this situation, but the knowledge was not a help to me or them. I didn't imagine for a second that I was in any danger of starving to death, but what if...? I had water, but a thought crossed my ever-increasingly paranoid mind: Was the water safe to drink? If the black Dust was falling nationwide, and

I had to assume it was, would it affect the water processing plants? I decided not to take the chance. The water looked clear enough, but boiling it would be a wise precaution.

The fourth day showed no let up. Like a silent shroud, the Dust fell. My enforced incarceration was beginning to weigh on me. Sleep was impossible; inactivity is sometimes more tiring than a long workout. I washed, showered, shaved, changed my clothes, and even made my bed. I wanted to try and keep up at least a rudimentary routine. It wasn't working. Even though I knew it was pointless, I continually checked my phone, fighting the frustration that welled up inside when I discovered the truth I already knew. Moving listlessly from room to room, the windows black with Dust, the all-pervading silence pressing in on me like a huge weight, claustrophobia nibbling at the edge of my composure, I felt like screaming.

Have you ever stood by an open fridge staring at the empty shelves as if food might somehow magically appear? I know I have; I did it then. The cheese was greener, the butter dish with barely a scrape left, which didn't matter as there was no bread. A third of a pint of milk in its plastic container was just about to turn. No tea, no coffee. I'd eaten the last two custard creams that morning for breakfast. The cupboards and refrigerator were as bare as Old Mother Hubbard's.

Chin on chest, I sighed heavily.

"Well, I could do with losing a few pounds..." I closed my eyes. Not funny.

I was due to get groceries at the end of the month. Like every other household, bachelor or not, toward the end of the month, supplies dwindled as grocery day approached. Just bad timing. The thought stirred, just a tickle at the back of my mind. Slowly, my chin rose and eyes narrowed, staring into the bright interior light of the empty fridge, groping for the revelation lingering just on the edge of realization...

"You stupid, fucking bastard..."

I suddenly became animated.

Mr. Bradbury... Mr. Bradbury! Every time I went into his small corner grocery store, he'd joke about me gaining weight.

"Too many custard creams, Adam?"

"T.V. dinners? You're turning into a couch potato."

Mr. Bradbury's corner shop was two doors down from the flat! How could I not remember that? I'd shopped there for over three years ever since I had taken on the flat, too lazy to go to the Tesco's in the high street.

"Idiot!"

Slamming the fridge door, I headed for the stairs, eager to get to the shop, only slowing, my hand on the banister when I realised the horrible truth. The shop was less than a hundred yards from my front door, but with the dark deluge outside, it might as well be a hundred miles. Thinking about it, I remembered the shop had steel security shutters over the door and windows. Even if I somehow managed to get there, I wouldn't be able to get in. My heart—and my stomach—sank, enthusiasm wilting, my mind desperately going over the possibilities. The shutters might not be down. Mr. Bradbury might have opened up before the Dust started to fall, and maybe he was trapped inside the store.

I thumped the banister. It was too risky. The shutters were probably down, and the possibility of becoming disorientated and lost was too great. I could chance following the wall, keep my hand in contact with the bricks, but if I tripped or blindly walked into something, a lamp post or rubbish bins...

"Bollocks."

I sat on the top step, my head in my hands. Tears stung the backs of my eyes, on the verge of crying in frustration. But I didn't. I had to think this through. There had to be a way to get into the shop.

A sudden idea had me hurrying to the kitchen. The window overlooked the back. I couldn't see anything, but I didn't need to. The rear access was a narrow alley running the length of the terraced houses culminating at the corner at the rear of the shop. I didn't know for certain, but I was guessing the security at the rear might not be as tight as the front. The point was I couldn't get disorientated in the alley no matter how thick the Dust was, and I could take extra precautions.

Pulling all my camping gear out of the large, built-in cupboard on the landing, I discarded the two rucksacks, my sleeping bag, two tarpaulins, and a small three-man tent, dumping it all on the floor behind me.

"Hah!" I yelled in triumph as I spied the two hanks of five fifty paracord, a thin, very strong cord with a thousand uses.

One hank was used with about fifty yards of cord left; the other was a full hundred yards, perfect for my purposes.

Rummaging further, I pulled out a pair of half-face swimming goggles. Taking my treasures to the kitchen, I put them on the table while I looked into the cupboard beneath the sink. I retrieved a used pack of decorating masks—the white polystyrene things—there were only three left, but I would only need one. That coupled with my scarf should keep the Dust out of my nose and throat.

Using a double fisherman's knot, I tied the two lengths of paracord together, winding it back into a single hank. I was almost done; all I needed was a hammer and chisel from my toolbox, a couple of plastic shopping bags, and I'd be ready.

Don't let my cocky self-assurance fool you. I was as nervous as a cat in a dog pound standing by the back door with the black Dust swirling all around me. I must have looked a sight with bright blue goggles and a grey scarf wrapped around my lower face, but I didn't give a shit. I secured one end of the paracord to the drainpipe just outside the back door, doing most of the work by touch as I couldn't see a damned thing. The hammer and chisel were in my belt, the shopping bags stashed inside my windcheater.

"Holy shit," I muttered as I stepped out of the door.

I was immediately disorientated. It was weird. The Dust was billowing, but I couldn't feel any wind. I realised I couldn't even feel the dust. There was a softness underfoot but no resistance as I carefully paid out the paracord behind me, tentatively crossing the small, paved back yard. After two steps, the back door was completely lost to sight, and I had a brief moment of panic, forcing myself to be calm and keep going.

The back gate was suddenly there. I fumbled around the leading edge, grateful to find the latch. The old wooden door creaked open, and I stepped into the alley beyond. The one thing I never liked was sense deprivation, blindfolds, or using earplugs to sleep, but this was worse. My eyes were open, but I could see nothing. My ears were unplugged, but I was deaf. It was unnerving. Easing my hold on my lifeline, which I was unconsciously gripping very tightly, I tried to visualize the alley and my way forward. There wasn't much to visualize. I'd walked it a hundred times.

Just turn right and walk.

My balance was affected as I had no visual point of reference, tending to overcompensate as I stumbled along in short, careful, pigeon steps. I cracked my shin twice on some unseen obstacle, a box or a crate—who knew? It was only then I saw a major flaw in my plan... How the hell would I know which back door belonged to the shop? I fumbled along the wall, peering closely at the first two back gates I came across, my face almost touching the cracked, peeling paint. There was no number or sign that informed me whose back door it was, and why would there be? A brief unsettling thought occurred to me: did the shop actually have a back door? I couldn't remember.

I stumbled into space. Alarmingly, the wall had disappeared beneath my questing fingers. I nearly shouted, my heart pounding in my ears, my breath coming in short sharp gasps. I remained still, not daring to move.

"Calm down! Calm down!" I repeated like a mantra.

Gathering the paracord in both hands, I started to reel it in, retracing my steps, grunting as my shoulder thumped against the corner of a brick wall.

"Okay..." I said. "The shop front is to my left, just past a short expanse of brick wall. The alley is in front which means, all things being equal, the first back door I reach should belong to the shop."

Talking out loud to myself was somehow reassuring. My logic seemed sound, but then, were all things equal? I sighed heavily: only one way to find out.

The door appeared sooner than expected, which gave me hope. I looped part of the paracord securely around my wrist and then began exploring the door. There were no padlocks, which made sense, but there was a heavy-duty deadbolt which supported my belief that this was the shop.

I banged on the door with the hammer. It sounded pretty solid. That didn't bode well. Continuing to bang and yell at the top of my voice, I hoped for some sort of response from Mr. Bradbury. All was silent. I located the approximate site of the deadbolt, placed the chisel, and began hammering the blade in, periodically shifting the chisel blade as the hammer struck home. After a few more hard blows, I examined the damage, or rather lack thereof.

"Shit, shit, shit!" The door was covered in a galvanized zinc sheet. "Shit!" I kicked the door in frustration.

I looked up, seeing nothing, somehow remembering the first part of the rear wall was strung with barbed wire. More of Mr. Bradbury's security. There was no way to get past that, especially under these circumstances. The door was my only option.

I don't know how long I hammered at that fucking door, but finally the thick wooden jamb succumbed. Sweating profusely, I stepped back. Measuring the distance by touch, I kicked at the door savagely, and with a loud cracking of tearing timber, it flew open. With both hands on either jamb, I stood in the doorway trying to pierce the space beyond. Now I really was blind. I had no idea of the layout of the shop's backyard. Crates, boxes, bottles—there could be any manner of obstacles, but it wasn't stopping me. Thrusting the hammer and chisel back into my belt, I gathered the paracord and inched forward.

Someone must have been smiling at me that day because I reached the back of the shop without incident. A quick, tactile examination revealed barred windows and another zinc-plated back door, this one with two deadbolts.

"Of course, it does," I said ruefully. I hit the top left-hand part of the door and kicked the lower left. The door didn't move. "With slide bolts top and bottom."

It was a vain hope, but I tried anyway, hammering on the door and yelling, making enough racket to wake the dead. Mr. Bradbury was definitely not at the shop. I set to work with the hammer and chisel, doing my best to ignore the constant fogging of the goggles and the uncomfortable trickle of sweat down my back and sides. I stopped now and then and kicked the door, but it was a steadfast bastard. Hats off to Mr. Bradbury's security acumen… Not!

I'm not sure if I was laughing at my joke or if I had become hysterical; regardless, I was hammering away and giggling like some demented dwarf mining in some dark cave until finally the door surrendered. Gratefully, I stumbled inside, my shoulders and arms burning with fatigue. Closing the door, I threw off my goggles and slid to the floor, my arse thumping onto the hessian mat. I could vaguely feel the hessian prickle my buttocks through my jeans, but I didn't have the strength just yet to move to a more comfortable position. Clawing the mask and scarf from my face, I took a deep, satisfying breath. I'd made it!

Mr. Bradbury wasn't home. I flicked on a light and made a quick tour of the rear of the shop dispelling any fears that he may have been lying unconscious somewhere. The small kitch-enette was neat and tidy with a kettle and a microwave, a sink in one corner, and a battered armchair in the other. Three very large chest freezers occupied a second room; a cursory glance revealed a treasure trove of frozen delights. I wondered how long they would stay frozen should the electricity supply fail, but I decided it was pointless worrying about it. I would go through the freezers and take whatever they yielded, leaving a note and payment on the small table by the armchair. I was confident Mr. Bradbury would understand. Right now, I had something else on my mind.

On my way to the main room in the shop, I passed a medium sized room, its shelves stacked with dry goods, pasta, rice, cereals, and the like. They would be useful in the long term, but what I wanted would be in the shop behind the counter on a shelf to the right. I flicked on the light and headed straight for them.

Custard creams. Heaven on Earth! The king of biscuits! The only thing missing was a cup of tea, a situation I would remedy as soon as I got back to the flat. As I packed the shop-ping bags, I was glad the shop did not have an alarm system. I guess Mr. Bradbury thought the security fortifications were enough, which under normal circumstances, I would agree. I also thought of staying in the shop.

It was going to be a trek getting back to the flat, especially loaded with full shopping bags, but somehow staying seemed an invasion, a step too far. I couldn't reconcile myself to the notion. The supplies would be convenient, but with only a microwave, my options would be very limited, and then there was the question of where to sleep… No, my flat was my best option. I would list everything I had taken. Mr. Bradbury knew me, and we would work it out. On the plus side, all the hard work was done, though breaking and entering was not my forte—as this little expedition clearly showed—the way was now open should I need to make further forays for supplies.

I also considered tying off the paracord leaving a perma-nent guideline for the duration of the precipitation, but what if it came loose or was somehow cut? Paranoia maybe, but I had no more rope…

The paracord was coming with me.

Three

November 2018

It was oddly pleasant riding through the silent town, the rabbits thrown across the handlebars of my bike, the rifle slung across my back. The wind rippled through my hair, cooling me, lifting it from my neck and shoulders as I coasted down Red Lion Hill, the tyres thrumming on the gritty asphalt. I enjoyed coming out here on my own, relishing the solitude, the peace and quiet. It was dangerous, but only if you forgot it was dangerous. Solitude had never been an issue for me. I often embraced it.

I loved to go camping, mainly on my own. Not the regular camp on a registered site with showers and toilets sort of camping but going into the wild places: Wales, Scotland, taking the bare minimum of equipment and supplies, relying on skill and living off the land. I didn't have a problem with people either, not really. I liked people, but that was mainly because I knew I could always walk away from them if I wanted to.

Things had changed. The world had changed, and I had to change with it if I expected to survive. It sounds all very dramatic, and I suppose it was, though at the time I didn't think of it like that...

Later that day, after the first foray to Mr. Bradbury's shop, getting back to the flat had been a mission, though having the promised tea and custard creams made it all worth it. I was sitting by the kitchen window on my third custard cream when I glanced out and I almost laughed...

Four

March 2018

"I don't fucking believe it!"

Continuing to stare through the glass, the custard cream in my hand forgotten, I realised I could see the houses across the alley. Not clearly, the Dust was still falling, but I could see them.

"Son of a bitch..."

I couldn't help but think it could have slowed earlier and saved all the aggravation of getting to the shop and back, but that's life. The view was the same from the front windows. I could see smudgy yellowed lights in the upper windows of some of the houses across the street like an impressionist painting. The street itself was a carpet of black, vague lumps dotted here and there, cars buried beneath the dust, the pavement invisible.

The Dust was thinning. I grabbed my windcheater and scarf and went downstairs. A pile of Dust tumbled into the hallway when I opened the front door. Kicking some of it out as I tied the scarf around my mouth, I stepped out into the street. Visibility was good; squinting against the light Dust still falling, I looked up and down the road. Curtains twitched in a couple of windows as people tentatively looked out, a mixture of relief and disbelief on shadowy faces. No one else ventured out into the street.

If it hadn't been bright red, I wouldn't have noticed the scarf, a splash of colour in a monochrome landscape by some wheelie bins thirty or forty yards away. I didn't know it was a scarf at that point; I peered closely, but it was hard to make out exactly what I was looking at.

"Here! Hey! Up here!"

The harsh, cockney voice distracted me; I turned to find the source.

"Up here, mate! Here! What's happening? Where'd all this dirt come from?"

The man was practically hanging out of an upstairs window. I couldn't make out details, but he looked drawn and haggard, his eyes dark-ringed, several days of stubble on his face.

"I've no idea," I shouted back. "I'm as wise as you are!"

"Haven't you heard anything on the news?" he called.

"Nothing. T.V. and radio are out. Have been from the start. No internet either."

"Same here," he said, crestfallen, obviously hoping for something more positive. "So, what is it? What's going on? I've never seen anything like this before."

"Like I said, I don't know, but it looks like it's stopping. My best advice is stay put. I'm sure the authorities have the situation in hand."

"Easy to say," he shouted. "We're out of food, and I've got kids in here!"

I glanced back at the scarf, something thin and pale was visible, maybe an arm...

"Look, give me a minute. I've got food. I'll bring some over."

"Well and good, but we need it now, mate. We haven't eaten for two days."

"Okay, okay, just give me a minute..."

The man continued to yell at me, but I wasn't listening. He wasn't happy. I checked that I could still see my front door before heading toward the red scarf. The Dust tickled my throat even though it was easing off. Using my hand as a shield for my eyes, I waded through black Dust foot deep. There was little resistance, but the Dust billowed as I trudged through it, almost enveloping me, hampering my advance if I moved too quickly. The red scarf resolved into a crouching figure, a woman wrapped in a dark coat huddled up against the bins.

"Oh man..."

I knelt beside her, brushing Dust away from her face. The red scarf covered her nose and mouth, framed by long hair full of the powdery downfall.

"Hello, can you hear me? Hey lady, talk to me!"

I pulled her into a sitting position. Her head lolled limply on her neck as Dust puffed between us. I couldn't see a thing. I needed to get her indoors to examine her properly. I got her into my arms; she was as light as a feather. I hoped this was her natural weight as I started across the street.

"Hey man! What about that food?" yelled the man in the window. "You just can't leave us to starve!"

"Food? Who's got food?" A woman's querulous voice sounded farther down the street.

"This guy here!" answered window man. "Says he's got food to spare."

"We need food! My babies are suffering, and we can't live on air and water!" A second woman's voice floated through the dust.

I ignored them. Heeling the front door shut, I staggered up the stairs to the living room, trailing Dust behind me. Carefully putting her on the sofa, I stripped off her scarf and removed her coat. She was pale and unresponsive as my fingers searched for the pulse at her throat. She was breathing, shallow, halting, her skin clammy. Getting a damp cloth, I wiped the Dust and grime from her face; it was caked around her mouth and nostrils. Her jeans and blouse were full of black dust, and it fell in drifts from her hair, settling on the sofa and floor.

Holding the back of her head, I tried to get her to take a few sips of water. Her lips were cracked and dry, her cheeks hollow; she was obviously suffering from dehydration. I guessed she was a few years younger than me, maybe early thirties. She was slim, attractive despite the haggard appearance; a wedding ring glittered on her left hand. *What the hell was she doing outside? Where is her husband?* Judging from the body odour, she hadn't washed in days. The smell was underlaid by the sharp tang of urine and something else I didn't want to think about.

"Hello, can you hear me?" I patted her hand as I held it in mine. "You're safe now. Hello?"

Suddenly, her eyes flew open, blazing bright blue; her arms flailed as she tried to get up from the sofa. I saw stars as a hand slapped me full in the face.

"Easy... Easy..." I gently restrained her by her shoulders. "You're safe now. It's okay, it's okay."

She grabbed my arm, digging her nails into the flesh, glaring at me in alarm.

"Where am I? How'd I get here? Who are you?" she croaked in a rush, immediately wracked by a harsh coughing fit.

I offered her the glass of water, and she emptied it in three quick gulps, gasping as the coughing fit subsided.

"I found you in the street. You were just about done in..." I began.

"The black dust? Street? What street?"

"Buckingham Avenue."

"Buckingham? Oh my God! How long have I been here?" She continued to look wildly about the flat, clinging painfully to my arm.

"Only a few minutes. The black Dust was stopping. I went out, saw your scarf. You were out cold."

"What day is it? Wednesday?"

Startled by the odd question, I said, "No, Friday. It's Friday, why?"

She sat up, confusion clouding her face, her movements short and quick. "It can't be. Three days... No..."

"I don't understand. What are you talking about?"

"Three days," she said, looking at me. "I left home on Wednesday..."

"You've been out there for three days?" I asked incredulously.

Her face worked as she sought to find answers. "I don't know. Wednesday, leaving the house... That's the last thing I remember."

"Where did you come from? Where's the house?" I asked.

"Stack Road. We just moved there. I was stranded, my car wouldn't start, and it was late..." Her words came all in a rush.

"Wait, wait, slow down. I don't understand. Why would you leave the safety of your home? You must have known it was dangerous. Where's your husband? Why isn't he with you?"

"There was nothing there: no lights, no food or water, nothing, just empty rooms."

Now I was really confused. "Look, you're not making sense. Maybe you need to eat, drink something, maybe get out of those clothes, and take a shower." I guess that was my way of diplomatically saying *you stink, lady*—ever the gentleman.

"I am hungry…" she said absently.

"Okay, let's get you some clean clothes. I've got some sweats you can use. They'll probably be a little big on you, but they're clean. The bathroom is there; I'll get you some towels."

"You have water?" she asked.

"Hot water," I smiled, "and electricity. I'll make you some soup while you shower."

Helping her to her feet, I held her for a second or two as she swayed dazedly.

"Do you think I could have another glass of water?" she asked, almost timidly.

"Of course." I got her some, and she drank it straight down again. "Adam," I said, taking the glass from her.

She looked a little surprised then managed a weak smile. "Linda," she answered.

"Thanks. I feel a lot better," Linda said, pushing the empty bowl away from her.

"You're welcome," I said. "D'you feel like talking?"

She shrugged, looking lost in the oversized grey tracksuit. "There's not much to tell," she answered wanly. "Rob, my husband, and I literally just bought a house on Stack Road. We closed last Saturday and got the keys. I took the week off so I could go there and sort out deliveries, having the amenities turned on and stuff. The gas and electric were supposed to be connected on Monday, but no one turned up. I waited all day, but nothing. Around seven, I decided to go back to the hotel and return the following day. Then the car wouldn't start. I haven't got A.A. or Green Flag, so I was stuck.

"We've just moved up from Hastings, so I don't know anyone in the area. Rob's firm relocated to Thurrock; he's an H.G.V. driver, long haul. Anyway, there was nothing I could do, so I called Rob, but he's in Ireland on a job. He suggested that I stay where I was until the morning and then try and find a local garage. So, that's what I did. I tried sleeping in the car, but it's a Mini and was really cramped; I didn't feel safe. Luckily, I had a car blanket and a couple of camp chairs. It wasn't exactly comfortable, but I managed. When I woke up just after dawn, I was greeted by the black dust. My phone didn't work, and I couldn't even see the car."

"What about neighbours? Couldn't they help?" I asked.

"I tried banging on the walls and shouting but got no response. I spent the whole day alone in an empty house with no amenities. All I had was a half-bottle of water. Wednesday came and I was tired, hungry, and scared. I decided to try and reach the neighbours. It was horrible. I put my scarf over my nose and mouth, but I couldn't see. I found a low garden wall, at least that's what I thought, but it led nowhere. By the time I realised I'd made a mis-take leaving the house, I was hopelessly lost. I... I panicked and began screaming for help. I thought I heard someone answering me. Stupidly, I ran towards the noise. I must have stepped off a kerb or something, and I fell headlong. I don't remember anything after that."

We sat and looked at each other over the kitchen table.

"I don't know what to say," I said quietly. "Three days out in that stuff must have been terrifying."

Linda shrugged. "Thankfully, memory loss can be a blessing sometimes." She shuddered as she continued, "I did get the feeling at one point that there was someone, or some-thing, out there with me. I couldn't see anything through the dust, but I felt it." She gave a little smile. "Paranoia..."

"Don't be so hard on yourself. I've had a taste of that too." I told her about my foray to Mr. Bradbury's shop. "So, there I was, hammering on the door and giggling like a lunatic, and that was only after thirty minutes out there. God alone knows how you must have felt. Oh shit!"

Linda blinked in surprise. "What?"

"The neighbours. I promised them some food." I rose from the table. "I'd better get some to them."

"I think you might want to look outside first," Linda said, nodding toward the window.

"Oh, for fuck's sake!"

The window was a black mirror, the Dust falling heavier than before.

"Do you think it will ever stop?" Linda's voice quavered.

"It has to," I said encouragingly.

I just wish I believed it.

"You're not married then?" Linda asked later that afternoon.

She'd slept most of the day. I guess it was some kind of escape for her.

"No, too much of a dreamer, I think," I said, clearing away our lunch plates from the table. "Never stood still long enough."

"Travelling?" she queried.

"No, not really. Though I spend a lot of time in the country," I said, sitting back down after putting the dishes in the sink. "Just had other things to do."

"Rob and me, we got married young, ten years now." The corners of her mouth twitched, her eyes wet.

"Try not to worry," I said. "I'm sure he's fine."

She looked at me as if I really knew. "You think so? He'll be so worried..."

"There's no way of knowing if the black Dust is just a local phenomenon or not. It's hard to imagine it could cover the entire U.K. I'm guessing there are far more people stuck outside than there are trapped in it. It's just a matter of waiting it out."

"Some may not have the luxury of time," Linda said.

I winced. "My neighbours..."

"Oh no! I didn't mean that!" She looked horror struck. "I wasn't judging you; it was just shitty luck. You would have helped them if you could."

"I should have helped them there and then; I'm thinking I still can," I said thoughtfully.

Linda frowned. "What are you talking about?"

"I've managed to get to Mr. Bradbury's shop, so maybe I can get across the street."

"NO!" Linda was on her feet, a terrified look of alarm on her face. "You can't! It's too dangerous, you'll... you'll get lost like I did. I can't be left alone again."

"Easy, easy, it'll be okay. There's two of us now, so you'll be able to watch my back, keep me safe."

"No, I was lost within minutes of leaving the house. I couldn't even find the car parked right outside. You can't risk it!"

I took her trembling body into my arms. She was shaking uncontrollably, clinging desperately to me as if I was going to rush out into the falling dust, leaving her lost and alone all over again.

"Listen, I've been out to the shop. I had enough rope to string across the alley, so I'd know when I reached the shop's back gate. I also ran a length of rope from the back gate to the back door of the shop; it made it a lot safer. You see? I take precautions, and I don't take needless risks. With you here, with your help, it will be even safer still."

"No," Linda protested, holding me tighter. "I won't be on my own again."

"You won't be. It's perfectly safe; I promise you." I eased her back and looked into her frightened eyes as I picked up the hank of paracord from the side. "I'll be tied to this," I began.

Linda touched the rope. "But it's so thin. What if it breaks?" she argued.

"It won't. Trust me. This is five fifty paracord; the five fifty means it can take the strain of five hundred and fifty pounds, almost unbreakable. It'll be tied securely around my waist, and you can stay at the front door and pay it out as I cross the road, keeping it taut so you'll know I'm still on the other end. I'll go straight across, keeping the line directly behind me, get to the neighbour's door, give them the food, and straight back. Simple."

Linda didn't look convinced.

"Come on. It'll be okay. You'll see. Just think we'll be helping those kids; they must be starving."

"He could have been lying. Maybe there aren't any kids."

I smiled inwardly at her last-ditch attempt to dissuade me. A twinge of pity touched my heart as I thought of the terror she must still be feeling.

"There are kids," I said gently. "I don't associate with my neighbours much, but I've seen the children coming and going. I have to do this. I can't in good conscience sit here eating when I know they are going hungry. You understand that, don't you?"

She nodded reluctantly, the fear still showing in her troubled eyes.

Five

March 2018

What do they say? *Seemed like a good idea at the time…*

"Christ!" The falling Dust was no longer a curtain but a wall of solid black. We couldn't even open the front door while I prepared to go out, just too much dust.

"You can't do this," Linda said worriedly. "Look at it out there; it's crazy."

I agreed, but I couldn't admit that to her. *I just keep seeing those kids.* There was no choice. I did think of another safeguard, or at least I thought I had. I retrieved my compass from the landing cupboard thinking I could plot a simple straight line, follow it out and back, and prevent getting lost. Turned out to be a no-go. I should have known it wouldn't be that simple. The Dust somehow affected the compass; it refused to settle down, the needle jig-jagging all around the dial, giving no clue as to true north. It was useless.

Of course, I didn't mention that to Linda either. What I did do was give her a whistle.

"A whistle?" She looked totally confused as I placed the small device in her hand.

"Yep, a whistle," I confirmed, probably unnecessarily. "It's louder, shriller, and takes far less energy than shouting. It's an important survival tool in the wild."

She thought I had lost my mind.

"I'm going in a straight line," I explained. "There and back. You blow that three times every few minutes, good, hard blasts, and I'll have an audio guide back to you."

I had both my rucksacks packed with food, one on my back the other across my chest. With the decorator's mask, scarf, and swimming goggles, I was just about ready with the added protection of a hoodie tied close about my head.

"Ready?" I asked. The look on her face told me she wasn't, but she nodded bravely. "Stand behind the door. Try to keep as much Dustout as possible. Keep the line taut. I'll be back before you know it."

I turned to the door, my heart pounding. With a last deep breath, I opened it and quickly stepped out into the deluge. It was as if a thick blanket had been thrown over me, instant silence, total black out. I squared my back to the door, looked straight ahead, and began to walk.

The Dust collected on my shoulders, my head, and on top of the rucksacks. The feel of it on my bare hands was distasteful, making my skin crawl. I continually shook my head, but it was pointless; it was falling way too fast.

I pushed on, the line tight behind me. As far as I could tell, I was maintaining a straight line, or at least I hoped I was. It seemed to take forever just to cross the road, and it was getting hard to breathe. The heavy downpour made oxygen scarce, something I hadn't even considered. My breathing was becoming laboured. I had to go faster, and suffocation was suddenly a distinct possibility.

"Wha...?" I froze.

Something had brushed past my left leg, touching the calf. It was impossible to see what. My mouth went dry; my tongue stuck to my palate as I remembered Linda telling me about something being out here. I laughed inwardly, thinking it was just a piece of rubbish blowing past, probably a newspaper or something.

I knew that was bullshit.

Bumping into the wall was a welcome relief. I stood for a second or two, breathing slow and shallow, deciding which way to go, left or right. I figured six steps to the left. If I didn't find a front door, then six steps right, and then another six. The door couldn't be much more than fifteen feet away in either direction.

It turned out easier than that—three steps and there was the door. I pounded on it, yelling, unsure if my shouts would be heard, but shouting anyway. I thought I heard muffled voices, but I wasn't sure. I pressed my ear to the door, continuing to pound with a clenched fist. After what seemed an age, the door opened, and I staggered in.

Before I could get my bearings, I was grabbed and thrust back against a wall. The goggles had steamed up, everything was a blur. I had a vague impression of a man brandishing a hammer looming in front of me, his face close to mine, twisted in a mixture of fear and anger. Over his shoulder I could barely make out another shape, a woman, huddled at the foot of some stairs, two young children clinging to her.

"What the fuck are you doing? Who are you? What do you want? You scared my kids half to death!"

It was an understatement to say that the man was panicked, overreacting.

"Food!" I shouted, scrabbling the mask from my mouth. "I've brought food!"

The man stepped away, uncertain. I let the rucksack across my chest drop to the floor, Dust billowing.

"Look," I said, unbuckling the top flap. A bag of rice and a few cans fell, rolling across the floor.

"Thank God!" the woman cried, rushing forward. She pulled open the rucksack's drawstrings revealing the culinary treasures inside. "Thank you, thank you!" She was almost crying. "Charlie look, look!"

Bewildered, the man looked at the food then back at me.

"I'm sorry," he stuttered. "I didn't mean to be so rough. Things are…"

"It's okay, I get it," I cut in, shrugging the rucksack off my back. "There's enough food there for three or four days, rice, pasta, cans. Your neighbour, the woman who's got the baby?"

"Tina," The man said. "She lives next door. That was you in the street earlier?" Charlie asked.

"Yeah, I would have been here sooner, didn't expect the Dust to start again."

"What the hell is that stuff? Where's it coming from?" Charlie asked.

"I really don't know," I answered. "Whatever it is, we're going to have to try and ride it out. The food should help."

"Yeah, yeah, thanks. You saved our lives," he said, running a hand through his thinning hair.

"I've got to get back; I've left a friend on her own and she'll worry. Can you get food to your neighbour, maybe others who might need it?"

"We'll pass it over the garden fence," said Charlie's wife with an armful of cans.

"Good," I said. "Look, I don't know how long this is going to go on for, but if it hasn't stopped in three days, I'll come back with more food.

"Maybe it might be a good idea if you and your family come across to mine, safety in numbers. I've got access to enough food for us all."

They looked at each other.

"I don't know," stammered Charlie's wife. "Going out there, my kids..."

I smiled encouragingly. "Don't worry. It probably won't come to that. If it does, then I'll bring food to you, no problem."

Charlie grabbed my hand. "Thanks, mate. You're a lifesaver."

"No prob," I said, a little embarrassed. "Just keep it together. I'm sure all this will be over soon."

Going back out of that door was the hardest thing I've ever done. Masked, somewhat lighter, I began the nightmare journey back across the street, reeling in the paracord as I went. The claustrophobic smothering of the Dust was oppressive. I've always considered myself strong-willed, resilient, but being immersed in this stuff sapped my will like some sort of sensory vampire. It drained me, leaving me feeling empty, alone.

The dulled sound of the whistle dispelled the melancholy insidiously creeping into my mind. I shook my head, casting away the negative thoughts. I began to smile, feeling my spirits lift. The whistle had been a good idea.

The line jerked in my hand, tugging once, twice.

"Okay Linda, I'm on my way."

My smile broadened, then faltered. The line went limp in my hand.

I stopped in my tracks, my heart missing a beat, a chill washing over my entire body. Forcing myself to stand still, not to turn, I began reeling in the paracord; it was loose, drooping from my fingers. Then I felt the end of the cord slip through my hands.

"Oh my God." It was barely a whisper, issued from a constricted throat tightening with fear.

For a few seconds I couldn't think; everything was blank. I had no idea how far I was across the road or how far I was from my front door.

"Linda! Linda, can you hear me?" I waited, praying for a reply. "Linda!"

Nothing.

Panic began to overtake me. I couldn't stay here—I knew that—I either had to go forward or make my way back to Charlie's. But I couldn't even see my tracks in the dust. My hands waving blindly in front of me, I edged forward.

Oh, sweet Jesus...

I stopped as disorientation threatened.

Dropping to one knee, I discovered I was kneeling in eighteen inches of black dust, the last place I wanted to be. I quickly stood up.

"Linda! Answer me! Linda!"

Still nothing.

One thought kept racing through my mind like a maniacal round robin. *Its five fifty paracord. It can't break; it's impossible. But it broke.* I didn't want to think of what that implied. My immediate problem was what to do now.

My first impulse was just to rush forward. I couldn't be more than twenty or twenty-five feet from the flat. Worst-case scenario, I would run into the wall. *What if I tripped or blundered into something? It would be so easy to lose all sense of orientation. Would going slower increase the risk of losing direction?*

My body tensed; I wasn't exactly sure what do, but I had to do something, and quick. I was hyperventilating, my chest hurt, gasping for breath. Then from slightly to my left, I heard the frantic, repetitive, shrill whistling. It was louder than before, closer, with a touch of panic reflecting in the short, sharp blasts.

"Linda, thank Christ," I said, confidently hurrying forward toward the blessed sound.

I can't describe the elation of reaching the wall, the front door inches away, the shrill whistle. I all but fell through the door as Linda's hands hauled on my jacket, pulling me in, the door slamming shut behind me.

"What happened?" Linda was nearly hysterical as I collapsed against the hall wall. "You said the rope couldn't break. You said it was impossible. I was terrified; I thought I'd lost you!"

"It's okay," I said, sweeping the hood back and pulling off the goggles. "You saved me, brought me home." I began coughing.

"You bastard! I was so scared." She looked exhausted. "The rope..."

I picked up both ends of the paracord, the cough still irritating my throat as a tingle crept up my spine. The paracord had been cut.

"How?" Linda asked when I told her.

"I don't know," I lied. "It must have caught on something sharp."

"Like what? There's nothing between here and there, no cars, nothing."

I didn't know what to tell her. I only remembered something brushed past me, something tugging on the rope, and then there was no rope.

"It doesn't matter now. I'm safe, thanks to you. For me that's a win-win situation. The neighbours have food, the kids can eat, and it's all good."

Linda glared at me. Saying nothing, she turned and went upstairs.

We ate in silence. I defrosted a couple of steaks, made some pasta, and opened a bottle of Merlot as a peace offering. I'd hoped to cheer her up, maybe bring a little normality into the situation. It was late, gone eleven, closer to midnight. It had been a long day, a long first day, but we were too amped up to sleep; though I knew as soon as I settled, I'd go out like a light.

"You okay?" I couldn't stand the silence anymore.

Linda looked at me from across the table. "I trusted you," she said quietly. "You said it would be all right. You could have gotten lost or worse."

"I know. I'm sorry, but I had to take the chance. I couldn't let those kids suffer anymore."

"I get that, I really do, but we don't know what we're dealing with, what's causing all this." She looked down at her hands hidden in her lap. "I'm scared."

"Me too," I confessed. "But there's not much we can do about it except try and get through, and the only way we're going to do that is by helping each other."

"I feel so isolated, cut off as if I was in a cocoon or a coffin. What if there is no end to this?"

"There will be. There has to be," I returned.

"But will we be here to see it?"

"Linda, you have got to stop thinking like this. We have to keep positive, the first rule of survival…"

"And you'd know about that?" she cut in.

"Actually," I said, "I would."

She looked surprised.

"It's sort of a hobby—or more of a lifestyle. Of course, my training is mainly intended for remote places: Wales or Scotland, camping, living off the land, building shelters. Unfortunately, it's not a lot of good in this situation, but the mental strength of positive thinking is. If we keep focused and positive, I promise we'll come out the other end."

She just looked at me agog.

"Sorry," I said somewhat abashed. "I'll get off my soapbox now."

Linda surprised me by suddenly laughing, not a mocking laugh, but a sincere, clear, fresh happy laugh.

"Well, that told me." Her laughter was infectious. "That's priceless. Adam, if I've got to be stranded all alone with someone in the middle of a Dust storm, I'm glad it's you!"

Then we were both laughing.

It had been a long time since I sat in quiet contentment with soft music, a glass of wine, and an attractive woman. The lights were low and the atmosphere intimate; under any other circumstances, the situation would have been perfect. I'll be honest and admit I had to continually remind myself that Linda was married and very vulnerable right now, and I was no predator. But it was good to forget, if only for a few hours, what was happening outside.

"So, what do you do for a living?" Linda asked from the other side of the sofa.

"I guess I'm in the same business as your husband, only on a smaller scale," I said. "I drive a black cab, except mine's white."

"White?"

"Yeah, I'm an independent; I can work when and where I please, allowing me to go camping as often as possible."

"That's what you meant about not being married?"

"Partially, I think I'm too selfish."

"After what you did today, I don't think *selfish* comes into it."

"That was different," I said, my cheeks reddening.

"And was coming out to get me 'different'?"

"Absolutely. I didn't know you were there." I suddenly felt myself becoming defensive. Opening up, showing my feelings, and talking about myself was foreign to me; it was not something I liked to do.

"So, you're saying that if you had seen me, you wouldn't have rescued me?" Linda chuckled at my discomfort. "Course you would," she laughed. "Sorry, I couldn't resist. You were looking so serious."

She made me laugh.

"Tell me about yourself. Have you any family?" Linda asked after a few moments.

"No, just me," I answered, trying to hide my blushes by sipping some wine. "Mum passed when I was young leaving just me and Dad. He passed a few years ago."

"Oh, I'm sorry," Linda said.

"Mum had me late in life. She was told she was one of those women who would find it difficult to conceive, difficult, but not impossible. After I was born, Mum was continually ill. She never was a strong woman to begin with according to Dad. Pneumonia took her just after my fifth birthday."

"Dad was a cabbie too. He spent thirty years behind the wheel; there wasn't a place in London he didn't know," I smiled, remembering. "We had this thing where I would think of a place, and he would tell me the quickest way to get there, even pointing out landmarks on the way. I thought once I became a cabbie, I would make it harder for him, but I never beat him once."

"Sounds like a good dad." Linda smiled.

"The best," I replied. "He worked long hours, mainly because I think he missed Mum. But he always had time for me, always there when I needed him. I couldn't have wished for a better..."

I stopped. "Did you hear that?" I said, cocking my head towards the open sitting room door.

"No," Linda said, sitting up. "What?"

I shushed her, listening.

"There it is again." I put my wine down and stood up. "I think there's someone at the front door."

Just as I reached the bottom of the stairs, Linda close behind, the knocking came again, soft, weak, followed by scratching.

"Shit! There is someone there!" I reached for the door handle.

"Adam! Stop!" Linda grabbed my arm. "Wait."

The knocking came again. I hesitated.

"Linda?"

She looked worried.

"It could be anyone out there," she whispered. "Why would anyone go out there in there first place?"

I looked at the door then back at Linda. "You did," I said emphatically.

Her faced creased. "Okay, I did, but this feels wrong. I can't explain. I just feel it."

Not really knowing what to do, I knelt behind the door, my fingers resting on the letterbox flap. My skin prickled, no doubt influenced by Linda's fear. Unconsciously holding my breath, I flicked the letterbox open.

Six

November 2018
THE BLOCK

Pedalling at a leisurely pace, I turned left at the bottom of Red Lion Hill; up ahead, I could see the glowing lights of the "Block," the place I now called home. A square, yellow bricked, two-story residential building which surrounded a small courtyard, the Block contained sixteen flats per floor, thirty-two flats in total: some one-bedroom, some two-bedroom, and the four on the lower east side of the Block were three-bedroom. The Taylor and Donovan families occupied two of these; they had kids. Of the twenty-nine people living in the Block, twelve were men, including me. Seven women and ten children, all between the ages of six and eighteen; six of the children were orphans.

The glow from the fire lit up the main arch leading into the central courtyard, the only means of access in or out of the Block, except for a small gate at the rear of the building. I freewheeled under the arch and into the courtyard. Shadows capered on the walls, cast by the fires set in the four oil drums in the middle of the square. Dark figures sat on boxes and deckchairs or stood quietly, often into the wee hours. Sometimes they talked in muted conversation, most times not. Mostly, they stared into the mesmeric flames, lost in their own thoughts.

"Adam! You're back!"

Smiling, I coasted to a stop beside the frail figure of an elderly black man swathed in a huge overcoat and scarf. His close-cropped hair was sprinkled with grey; his dark, intelligent eyes sparkled in a square-lined face.

"Jules!" I greeted, pretending not to notice that he was trying to hide his anxious expression caused by my long absence.

"And bearing gifts I see!" he beamed, spying the rabbits.

"I'll take those." A woman appeared out of the shadows, the firelight shimmering in her shoulder-length red hair.

"I wouldn't trust them with anyone else, Sally," I said, handing the rabbits over.

Sally took them, hooking them onto her chubby fingers as she turned and pranced away. "You don't know what I'm going to do with them yet," she threw back.

"It can only be good," I countered.

Sally laughed and blew me a kiss as she disappeared into her flat. Five foot two, flaming red hair, plumpish, forever cheerful, with mischievous blue eyes, Sally had the God-given gift of doing marvellous things with food, from Spam to lobster, not that we ever saw much lobster!

"Stew," Jules said emphatically.

"Nah, spit-roasted with B.B.Q. sauce," I said, turning back to him.

We laughed.

I watched as Jules waved at a single-decker bus parked to the right of the arch. The engine thundered as it pulled forward, covering the entrance completely; the side closest to the arch was heavily armoured with double thick corrugated iron sheets.

"Right, I need to clean up," I said, feeling suddenly tired. "Get out of these clothes."

"You okay?" Jules asked, frowning.

"Yeah, I'm good. Been a long day."

I could feel the old man's eyes boring into my back as I wheeled my bike across the courtyard. He knew something was wrong, and he also knew now was not the time and place to discuss it. I nodded at one or two of the people seated around the fires; Tom Taylor and his eldest son, Andrew, one of three, waved at me through the thick cloud of wood smoke. Teresa Wright was sitting on an old tea chest nursing a bottle of beer; she was early thirties, attractive, quiet. She gave the barest of nods as I passed.

Leaving my bike out of the way at the foot of the stairs, I got to my flat. I was the only resident who opted for first floor accommodations, but it seemed safer somehow. Propping my rifle against the hall wall and stripping off my weapons belt, I sighed with relief. Holding my knife and axe in my hands, I paused. The knife was a heavy-bladed Schrade 56, razor sharp, black powdered, great for survival in the wild.

It was the axe that gave me pause; it was just a run of the mill hatchet I'd picked up at some hardware store or other months ago. It replaced my Gransfor-Bruk forest axe, a beautiful piece of kit. It reminded me of what might have been, but at least I knew the axe had gone to a good home.

I sighed again as I put my Glock on the dresser, close to hand. I was becoming maudlin. A shower would remedy that. Quick and cold, but it made me feel a thousand times better, more alive. Beer and clean clothes, in that order, would be better still.

I took the beer and my Glock up to the roof. It was a quiet place, my place. London lay in darkness to the north, the southeast and east part of the city were clearly visible, even in the darkness. In my head, I saw Greenwich, Deptford, and Woolwich as they used to be, the London I knew growing up. Here and there, tiny sparks of flame highlighted the buildings, fires like the ones below, probably also set in oil drums. Most of the city was dead, but there were people out there. Survivors, like us, trapped, like us.

I heard a grunt and the scuffle of boots on the roof gravel. I knew who it was without turning.

"You okay, Old Man? Thought I'd be safe from you up here."

Jules chuckled, a deep rich sound. "I may be getting on, but I can still climb a damned ladder."

We stood together in silence looking out over an empty city.

"Is it bad?"

There was no point in lying. "It's real bad, Jules," I said quietly. "The east side of the park is completely overrun, the lake bridge is gone, the vines are spreading fast, and they're almost to the high street."

"Damn," Jules said.

"It gets worse," I continued. "Shooters Hill is barely passable. A week, maybe less, it will be gone. Oxleas Wood, the Common, Herbert Pavilions ... gone. Several roads are breaking up: Academy Road, Woolwich Road, the top of Red Lion Hill, concrete and tarmac cracking."

"Subsidence?" Jules queried.

"No, the ground is being pushed up, not sinking. I think the vines are sending out subterranean roots like blackthorn; there's no way of knowing where they will surface."

"How long?" he asked.

"Before we get completely cut off? I figure two months, maybe three."

"And before they reach us?"

"Does it matter? Once we have no means of escape, it just becomes a matter of time. It'll be a question of what comes first: we run out of supplies or we're overrun."

"Sweet mercy." Jules fell silent. After a few minutes, he said, "What we gonna do?"

I shrugged. "Go with the plan I guess, though I think it's just delaying the inevitable. If moving is our only option, we need to find somewhere completely safe, a permanent home. To be honest, Jules, I have no idea where that is."

He stood pensively for the longest time, chewing on his bottom lip. Then, sighing heavily, he turned to me. "Then I guess we better find somewhere before it really gets bad."

Bad. Yeah, I can remember when things went bad...

Seven

March 2018
CREEPS

The exterior letterbox flap was snatched from my fingers. Before I even had a chance to cry out in alarm, I found myself staring into a pair of red and black eyes. For a long moment, I was paralyzed, unable to tear my gaze away, caught in the hypnotic glare of those inhuman orbs; I felt like I was falling into their turbulent depths.

Black Dust flew through the open letterbox, blinding me. It stung my eyes as I tumbled backwards, grunting as I landed heavily. Through watering vision, I saw the eyes still blazing, then the flap plonked shut; they were gone.

"Adam!" Linda was kneeling beside me as I rubbed at my eyes. "What is it? What did you see?"

Tears streaming down my face, I kept blinking until my vision slowly cleared. "We need to get upstairs," I said after Linda helped me to my feet. "Now."

Ushering her upstairs, I threw the bolts on the front door and followed.

"Eyes?" Linda said.

"Red eyes," I answered, taking a long slim case down off the bedroom wardrobe.

Linda was sitting on the bed watching me as I put the case down beside her and began unzipping it.

"What was it? A dog or something?"

"It was no dog. They weren't like any eyes I've ever seen outside a Dracula movie."

I pulled the contents out of the case; Linda gasped.

"Is that real?" she said, looking wide-eyed at the rifle in my hands.

"It's an L96 air rifle, .25 calibre; I use it for hunting small game when I go wild camping."

"Jesus, Adam," Linda said as I began to load the rifle.

"You didn't see those eyes, Linda. They were mad eyes, insane. I don't know what it was or how it's surviving out there in the dust, but it's there, and I don't think it's friendly."

"You're serious?" she asked incredulously.

"Absolutely," I answered, going to the hall cupboard.

I brought out a large, green canvas bag and set it down on the bed next to the rifle.

"Whatever's going on just took a turn for the worse," I said, unpacking the bag. "We need to be prepared."

I arranged the things from the bag on the bed. My black leather possibles pouch contained fire-lighting tools, a folding buck knife, compass, a black leather utility belt, a Shrade 56 hunting knife, a Gransfor-Bruk forest axe, and lastly, a Mora bushcraft knife.

"Okay," I said, seeing Linda's puzzled expression. "This is stuff I take camping, mainly in Scotland. Wild camping— that's camping anywhere you like—is illegal in England and Wales, but Scotland has a 'right to roam' rule which means you can camp anywhere as long as you leave the site the same way you found it. I'm telling you this because I don't want you thinking I'm some sort of survivalist nutjob with a house full of random weapons."

"You could have fooled me," Linda said shakily.

I smiled. "These aren't weapons, Linda. They're tools used to make living off the land easier and put a zing into camping."

"Not to mention fending off red-eyed beasties, I'm guessing."

"Exactly," I said, picking up the axe and Mora knife. "These are very sharp, and I want you to keep them close to you, just in case."

"You're kidding me, right?" Linda said, looking aghast at the offered tools. "I'm no good with this sort of thing!"

"You won't need to be. I'm just hedging my bets here, worst-case scenario." I sat on the bed next to her. "Listen, I might be overreacting a little, but those eyes were real, very real; I can't impress that on you enough. When this Dust stops, I've no idea what we'll find outside, and I'm not about to take chances. It's probably nothing. Like you said, it might've been a dog driven crazy by the dust. Who knows? But I want to make sure. Just keep them close, that's all."

The world has changed and not for the better. It was late, gone midnight, and we were both tired. I gave the bed to Linda; fortunately, I have a very comfortable sofa.

I didn't think I was going to sleep; those eyes haunted me. I lay with a sleeping bag over myself and began to doubt my own senses. I figured the Dust was some sort of weather anomaly. I didn't know the how or why of it, but what else could it be? But now, after seeing those eyes, crazy thoughts were swimming in my head.

"Adam?" Linda's silhouette was visible in the bedroom doorway. "I don't want to be alone."

She padded over, still dressed in the grey tracksuit and trailing a blanket. I slid over, making room for her, and she got on the sofa beside me, covering herself with the blanket. I put a protective arm around her, and we slept.

The Dust fell for three more days. And then it didn't.

It just stopped. I didn't actually see it stop; I just looked out of the kitchen window early Saturday morning and saw blue sky and houses.

"Adam!" Linda called from the living room.

"I can see," I called back.

We met at the top of the stairs, and she eyed the rifle in my hand.

"Just a precaution," I assured her.

Now that we could see outside, everything was black from the aftermath of the dust. I opened the door and a large pile of it collapsed inward, throwing up a fine cloud.

"Adam…" Linda indicated the base of the door.

The paintwork was scratched with claw marks, four lines criss-crossing across the wood, deep gouges marking the lower panels.

"Shit," I breathed. "Not a word to anyone until we can figure this out," I said.

Linda nodded, shaken by the scratches.

Keeping the rifle down by my leg as inconspicuously as possible, I went out into the street. The sky was clear, the bright blue making me squint against the light. Everywhere was coated with dust; it must have been two feet deep. Wading through it was easy if we moved slowly. A door opposite us opened, and Charlie stepped out, blinking in the sunlight. He waved.

"Is it over?" he called.

"I think so," I called back. "Just don't go too far from your front door, just in case."

More people made cautious appearances. Some looked bewildered, others afraid; the women stayed close to their front doors while the men waded out into the street. They reminded me of sheep as they came together in the middle of the road, looking bewildered, milling around aimlessly. Several men ploughed through the dust, causing it to rise and fill the air with choking clouds as they futilely waved their arms in an effort to dispel it. I steered away from them.

"Jesus, I didn't think it was ever going to stop," Charlie said.

"I was beginning to wonder," I replied. "Is your family okay?"

"Yeah, fine, thanks to you. I figured the heavy downfall prevented you from getting back to us, but Julie, my missus, stretched out the food and made sure we had enough to see us through. We were fine."

"Good, I was worried," I said.

"No need. The question is, what now? Look at this stuff; it's everywhere. How the hell do we even begin to clear it up?"

"Charlie," I said, "I have absolutely no idea."

We were moving slowly towards the south end of the street. With the Dust so deep, walking any distance would be a nightmare. Cars might start, but the Dust was so fine it wouldn't take long for it to clog the engine. Of course, it begged the question: Even if we could clear it, what would we do with it all? Looking at the surrounding rooftops, tiny waterfalls of Dust were trickling down into the street. The sloping roofs were laden with the stuff; it coated every flat surface, walls, windowsills, and looked like an impossible task.

Raised voices at the end of the road caught my attention. Three men were standing by the small roundabout situated there. The roundabout was meant to ease congestion coming off the main A2 motorway that ran alongside Wellingham, and it never worked. If anything, it made things worse. Traffic was always bad, both in the morning and evening rush hours.

"How's that even possible?" said one of the men, a tall, thin man with a receding hairline.

"Well, seeing is believing," said another.

"Bloody odd if you ask me," retorted the first man.

The roundabout was about fifty feet in diameter and sat in the centre of the junction. The wet grass gleamed in the early morning light; not a single grain of black Dust was evident.

"Now that's peculiar," muttered Charlie.

The black Dust formed a perfect perimeter around the green island, an oasis in a black desert. Moving forward, I scooped up a handful of Dust and threw it onto the grass. It hung in the air for a few seconds then descended onto the green island and disappeared straight into the earth like a sponge soaking up water. None of the front gardens across the road showed any evidence of the dust; patches of green dotted the street. Across the roundabout, The Falcon pub had massive flowerpots either side of the entrance; closer inspection showed there was no Dust there either.

There was no explanation, at least none that I could see. I didn't know why the Dust wouldn't settle on bare earth and grass, but I didn't like it. It didn't make sense.

"It's a mess," Linda said.

"I'd have to agree on that," I replied, looking around at the gathering crowd. "Some of these people are still dazed, frightened. We need to do something."

"What?" Linda asked. "We've no resources; there's no way we can deal with this on our own."

"They must need food. Let's get some of them together, form a supply run. There's not enough to feed them all indefinitely, but there's food for a few good meals at Bradbury's if we ration it out."

"I'm not sure he'll be happy about that," Linda said. "Who's going to pay for it?"

"It's gone beyond cost, Linda. These people need help until proper aid arrives. I checked my mobile, service is still down, and I'm guessing there's a lot more people around the neighbourhood in the same boat. It could be days before help gets here, so we'll have to feed them ourselves as best we can for the moment."

Clicking her tongue and looking worried, she clearly didn't like the situation one bit, but she nodded nonetheless.

"Charlie?"

"Whatever needs to be done," he said.

People were hungry and confused. One or two were belligerent, blaming the government for all sorts of things from failed nuclear experiments to global warming. The thought of food brought them all together.

"How do we get into the shop?" asked Michael, a big, buff man with a thick beard. He was one of the belligerent ones. "Ol' Bradbury's got the place more fortified than Fort Knox."

"The back's open. We'll get in that way, assess what food there is, and distribute accordingly," I suggested.

"It's not going to feed the whole street," protested Michael.

I knew straight away he was going to be trouble, but the last thing I wanted was a panic on my hands. He was big, but he was also carrying a very expensive beer belly. I got the impression that Michael normally got what he wanted in his household.

"There'll be plenty, enough for everyone if we distribute fairly," I assured him.

"Some of us need more than others; I'm a big man, I got diabetes, I need to eat."

"The kids need to eat, too," said Tina, Charlie's neighbour. "Their needs come first."

"I got kids, too," Michael came back.

"Look," I cut in, "let's just see what there is on offer first, shall we? Then we'll take it from there."

Michael mumbled something into his beard, but I didn't catch it.

"I think the best thing to do is use the shop as a way station. We work out what food we have and ration accordingly, starting with families with kids."

Charlie and Linda agreed.

"Okay, then let's get it done," I said, heading for the shop.

The provisions in the shop were basic but adequate, more than enough to go around. There was plenty of pasta, rice, cereals, plus boxes of canned goods. That was without counting the food already out on the shelves. Linda found a lot of ready-made frozen dinners in one of the freezers, which gave a little variety, if not a good diet. Most of the inhabitants of the street helped out, kept orderly lines, even brought bags to carry the food. Laughing and joking helped things go well.

"Adam…" Linda caught my attention, nodding across the shop.

Michael was loading up a large laundry bag with sweets, chocolate, and cigarettes.

"Dammit…" I swore under my breath.

I left Charlie and Linda to continue rationing food.

"Michael, what are you doing?" I asked.

Without turning, he continued to fill the bag. "Getting supplies. What d'you think?"

"Necessities man, the bare minimum to get by; you don't need any of that stuff."

"I got needs; so have my kids." He threw the bag over his shoulder.

"You'll be paying for that stuff then?" I asked reasonably.

"You're having a laugh, ain't you? This is an emergency situation."

"No, this is looting." I was beginning to get angry. "Your kids can go without sweets, and you're not going to tell me they smoke?"

Michael stopped what he was doing and looked at me, an ugly snarl on his lips.

"Who died and made you chief?" he grated.

"I'm just saying you don't need that stuff. As it is, we're imposing on Mr. Bradbury's livelihood, and I intend to make sure he gets paid for everything we're taking. Are you going to do the same?"

"Fuck you! You don't tell me what to do!" The big man turned on me.

"Maybe not, but he's right and you know it, Mike. Put it back." Charlie was a welcome sight.

Michael hesitated.

"I mean it, Mike," Charlie said evenly.

With rage twisting his face, Michael dumped the bag onto the floor and stomped past us.

"Fuck both of you!" he spat as he left the shop.

I sighed with relief. "Thanks. I thought that was going to turn nasty," I said.

Charlie just grinned at me. "What? Mike? Nah, he's an arse, all piss and wind. Anyway, you could have shot him."

I'd forgotten about the rifle slung across my back.

Two hours later, we were done. I left a note for Mr. Bradbury assuming total responsibility for the goods taken from his shop. I hoped he would understand. I thought he would. I pulled the back door and went out into the alley. Linda was waiting for me; a large brown carton was at her feet.

"I thought we could use these," she said, offering me a red and blue box.

"Bin bags?" I asked.

"Bin bags," she agreed. "Maybe if everyone clears the area immediately outside their homes, we can at least make the pavements passable."

I grinned at her. "Not just a pretty face then."

Picking up the carton, we went out into the street.

By early afternoon everyone was outside, rigged out in makeshift protective clothing and masks, filling plastic bin bags with black Dust and stacking them kerbside. It was a weird sight, but it raised morale. They had something to do, something constructive until help arrived, which I sincerely hoped wouldn't be too long. It would be good to get some qualified answers.

I made a late lunch while Linda showered. I needed to shower too after doing my bit bagging the dust, but ever the gentleman. We sat down to chicken noodle soup and fresh baked bread rolls. We'd found quite a stock of them in another freezer, the half-baked kind which you shoved into the oven for twenty minutes and presto, fresh bread.

"I'm going to Stack Road," Linda announced suddenly.

I felt something lurch inside me.

"You sure that's a good idea?" I asked, trying my best to be nonchalant.

She explained, "Rob might be looking for me. When he doesn't find me at the hotel, he'll go to the house."

"Of course, he'll be worried. He'll need to know you're okay."

The silence was a little awkward.

"It would be good if we could still be friends," she ventured.

I put down my spoon and fork and looked at her. "Linda, we are friends and I'd like to meet Rob, let him know he's a lucky man. But I was thinking more about the thing at the letterbox; we still don't know what it was or where it might be."

"I don't think it's a problem. We've been outside all day and haven't seen sign of any animals, even cats and dogs. I'm sure I'll be all right."

"At least take the axe and Mora knife; it would make me feel better. I could come with you?"

Her smile was winsome. "I don't think that's a good idea. I'm a couple of miles away. I'll go see if Rob's been there. I'll wait a bit, and if he doesn't show, I'll leave a note with this address and come back. Then maybe I'll let you take me to the hotel in your white taxi."

"Okay," I laughed, placated but not really happy. "Just be careful."

"I will. Don't worry."

I retrieved my backpacks from Charlie and packed one with some food and bottled water, plus my axe and Mora just to be on the safe side. Tina, Charlie's neighbour, had kindly lent Linda some clothes since they were about the same size. I told Linda she should carry the axe for easy access.

"You definitely worry too much," she said, kissing me on the cheek. "I'll be fine. Even if Rob is there, we'll come back to return your *tools* and backpack and let you know all's well."

We hugged and I walked her to the end of the road. I was going to insist on going with her, but she wasn't having it. Watching from the corner, I waited until she was out of sight. In blue jeans and a red hoodie, she was leaving just as she arrived, a bright splash of colour in a drab landscape. She waved, I waved back, and then she was gone.

Eight

November 2018

"So, where?" Jules asked.

It was a beautiful night, warm, a soft breeze cooling my skin as I looked south towards Bexleyheath and Dartford. I knew they were there, though I couldn't see any sign of the urban towns in the darkness. I didn't need to see them to know they had been overrun by the vines: thick, purple-black tendrils with white two-inch thorns which dripped lethal venom. They snaked out and clung to every surface, slowly crushing the life out of everything they came in contact with. A hideous jungle growing and spreading at a supernatural pace, killing everything in its path—with it came the Creeps, red-eyed beasties.

"I don't know, Jules," I answered wearily. "Thamesmead seemed a good choice, get to the northern sector, the industrial parks. With the River Thames at our back, I thought we could stem the spread of the vines before they took hold, build defences..." I trailed off.

"But?" Jules persisted.

"Same old problem," I said. "Supplies."

"We could use the river, use boats to scavenge along both banks," Jules suggested.

"That's what I intended," I explained, "but it's still limited." I sipped at my beer. "It all comes down to time, mate. Eventually supplies will run out, and we'd be going

farther and farther afield to scavenge until there would be nothing left."

"That's a pretty bleak outlook." Jules rubbed at his greying hair. "Pretty damned bleak."

"I can't see any alternative." I sighed. "We'll have to move, got to, probably to Thamesmead while we still can. Maybe gain some time, six months, maybe even a year until we can figure something better."

"So, when are we going to go? If things are as bad as you say, then it's gotta be soon."

"Yeah, but we can't just blindly go rushing off to Thamesmead. We've got no idea what the conditions are like there; it could be worse than here. I'm only going on the supposition that all the concrete there will have retarded the vines, but I don't really know."

"What are you saying?"

"That I need go look."

"That's crazy!" Jules was horrified.

"No crazier than staying here," I said. "Think about it: we can't take everyone to Thamesmead without first checking it out. Once we leave here, there's no going back. Look what happened the last time I went dashing off without thinking."

"It brought you to us," Jules said.

"It damned near killed me, that's what it did!" I returned hotly. "Too close for comfort. No, this time we look before leaping."

Nine

April 2018
WELLINGHAM

I was tired but somehow felt it was my responsibility to check how things were in the street, make sure the neighbours were okay. It's funny really, I lived for three years in my flat, barely on nodding terms with them; suddenly, we were thrown together amidst a shared disaster, and I was acting like a mother hen. I didn't quite know why.

Walking down the cleared pavement, I saw the bags of Dust piled against the kerbside forming a low wall, preventing the Dust still in the road from spreading. One or two women were putting the finishing touches to the cleaning, sweeping down windowsills and dumping what they had collected into the road. Night was falling, the street was quiet, and lights glowed in several windows.

Tomorrow, I planned to check the Falcon pub to see how they were faring, and maybe go down one or two of the neighbouring streets. No one dared to go too far from their homes, which was understandable, but I believed the worst of it was over. Services would soon be restored, communication would be up again, and things would start to get back to normal. Whether or not we would get any answers was another matter. Right then, I didn't care. I wanted to eat and shower. I would deal with tomorrow when it got here.

"Adam!" Charlie waved from his front door. "You okay?"

"Fine, Charlie. Just going home to eat," I called back.

"Come eat with us. There's plenty," he invited.

I almost declined but suddenly thought a little company might be nice. "You sure?" I queried.

"Absolutely! Come on. It's nearly ready."

I'm glad I accepted. Spaghetti Bolognese and some of those fresh baked rolls were served, but it was the ice-cold Sol beer that I really appreciated. Sitting around the family table, Charlie, Julie, and the two kids, David and Juney, were talking and laughing without a care in the world. It was as if the last week never happened. Charlie had an open fire in his living room, a rare thing in these days of air conditioning and central heating. Using smokeless coal and clearing out ashes from a cold grate was not for the new generation.

"Love a fire," Charlie enthused, sitting in one of two comfortable recliner chairs. I sat in the other. "Always thought it was the centre of any home."

"I thought that was the kitchen," I remarked, sipping my second beer.

"The kitchen is where all the work gets done!" chirped in Julie from the dining table as she sat reading a magazine.

"Don't give me that. You love it," Charlie said, winking at her.

For a moment, I felt something tug inside me. Charlie and his wife were in their early forties. He was a tall man, wiry, with the sort of physique that was a lot tougher than it looked. He wore his receding, fair hair short, was clean-shaven, and had eyes you instinctively knew you could trust. Julie was slim, had lively green eyes, and a foaming cascade of dark hair reached the middle of her back. They were a close-knit family; I envied them. Family life was not for me; there was so much still to do, so many things to see and experience. I didn't think I'd have the time. Seeing Charlie and Julie's familiar good-natured banter made me wonder. *What about later life?*

"I think I'm going to take my leave," I said, finishing my beer. "It's been a long week."

Charlie stood up and laughed. "Now there's an understatement, but at least it's over now, bar the clearing up."

"I think we made a good start today. It'll all work out."

I thanked them for dinner and the company. Calling out "goodbye" to the kids playing in their rooms, I went home.

A crash of thunder shook the whole house, snapping me out of a deep sleep and scaring the hell out of me. Still dazed, I leapt out of bed and rushed to the window. Dawn was breaking, but the sky was as black as sin. A few people were milling about in the street in their nightclothes and pyjamas, looking up at the early morning sky.

I spotted Charlie hanging out of his window. Throwing on some clothes, I hurried out just as lightning blazed. People ducked and a woman screamed as the crackling bolt was so vivid and prolonged. A mass of turbulent clouds roiled in a bruised sky, massive thunderheads from horizon to horizon, purple-black monsters threatening to fall and crush the earth.

"For fuck's sake! Isn't this ever going to end?" Charlie shouted over the rising wind as he came out his front door, struggling into a jacket over his track suit. "Haven't we been through enough?"

"This is mad!" I shouted back. "The whole world's gone crazy!"

More lightning blazed. The ground reverberated as thunder roared.

"Go back indoors, Charlie. I don't think it's safe out here!"

"You don't have to tell me twice. Come with me."

"No, I'm good. I'm going to try and get these people off the street."

"I'll help..." Charlie began.

"No, you've got a family to look after. Go!"

He hesitated, then reluctantly returned indoors whilst I shouted at the remaining people gawping at the raging sky to get to safety. The wind was picking up, getting stronger. Dust was lifted from the road and began to fill the air, blinding me. Someone barged into me; I turned and through watering eyes saw Michael glaring at me.

"What the hell are you doing? Get off the street! This storm's about to break!" I shouted.

"Fuck that and fuck you. I'm getting more supplies. I'm not getting caught short again!" he shouted back.

"That's crazy! You've got more than enough; go home and get safe!"

"I told you I don't have to listen to you. Get out of my fucking way!" He pushed past me, and I quickly lost sight of him in the blinding wind-blown dust.

Dammit!

I hesitated, thinking to go after him, then the first rain began to fall, huge, heavy droplets that soon turned into a deluge. I ran for home.

Slamming the door, I leaned back gasping, wiping the water from my face with my hand. Rain pounded on the front door as the skies opened up, and the storm broke in earnest. Within seconds, rain sheeted down in torrents. Lightning blazed, lighting up the cauldron of the sky in bright relief; thunder rolled, making the very ground tremble.

"Jesus..." I breathed.

From the living room window, I saw the world blotted out by a storm of biblical proportions, savage, violent, terrifying. I shivered and it wasn't entirely from the sudden cold gripping my body. Normally I loved a storm, enjoyed watching it rage and roar, the lightning, the thunder. It was a beautiful and terrifying thing to see. In the past, I had gotten out of bed in the middle of the night to witness nature's fury; her power stirred something primeval within me.

But this storm didn't feel right. It felt threatening, oppressive, as if it wasn't part of nature, but trying to destroy it.

My bedside clock read 4:45.

For two days, the storm was ferocious. Rain clattered against the window glass, thunder shook the doors and the pictures on the wall, and lightning ripped the darkling sky. Once again, I was trapped in my flat. My thoughts went back to the freak weather scenario, and the sudden violence of the storm gave weight to that theory.

What the hell is happening to the world?

Like the dust, the rain stopped as suddenly as it started. Mid-day Tuesday, it just ceased raining as if God turned off a faucet. The street was clear; barely any sign of the black Dust remained. The black bin bags lining the pavement were split and deflated, the contents entirely washed away.

"Well, that solves one problem," Tina Mitchell said, standing on the pavement outside her door.

"A blessing in disguise," agreed Julie.

I guess it was. The roads were clear, so I'd be able to get the taxi to find out what'd been happening elsewhere in Wellingham.

"D'you think the shops in the high street will be open?" Tina wondered.

"I'll get the car," Charlie said, almost as if he had read my mind.

"I wouldn't hold out any hope just yet," I said, "but it can't do any harm to go look. I'll come with you if that's okay?"

"Welcome the company," Charlie said. "Hang on here. I won't be a minute."

The avenue was comprised mainly of terraced houses built in the thirties when cars were few and far between. The roads were narrow and the pavements for pedestrians were wide, unlike some of the surrounding streets that had semi-detached houses with driveways on broad streets. Parking was extremely limited, which is why I garaged the taxi in a local covered lot at the end of Northumberland Avenue. The garages allocated to the houses were at the other end of the street behind the Falcon pub.

Charlie pulled around in a dark grey Ford Focus.

"Your chariot awaits!" he grinned, leaning out of the driver's window.

I opened the passenger door just as a worried looking woman came hurrying up, breathing heavily, her round face red and sweaty from the exertion of trying to run, not a good thing if you're overweight.

"Charlie! Charlie, wait!" she puffed, her hands holding onto her ample bosom, the blue mac she wore flapping out behind her.

Charlie got out of the car.

"Dot, what is it? What's wrong?" Concern creased his face.

Dot fought for breath as she tried to explain. "Michael, have you seen him? Is he here?" she gasped.

"No, Dot, he's not here. I haven't seen him since before the storm," Charlie told her.

Her expression was pained. "Oh my God, where is he? He went out just as the storm started, and he didn't come home. I thought he might have got caught and sheltered with you or someone."

"I'm sorry, Dot. I've no idea where he is," Charlie said.

"I do," I said. "At least I know where he was going just as the storm broke. Bradbury's."

"Bradbury's? That bloody, stupid man. I told him a few bars of chocolate wasn't worth the risk of getting drenched!" Dot wailed.

"Look, stay here with Julie," Charlie said, motioning his to his wife who came forward and put a comforting arm around the distraught woman's shoulders. "I'll go check Bradbury's. Mike's probably fallen asleep or something. Go with Julie, have a cup a tea, and we'll be back before you know it."

Julie nodded, and with some words of encouragement, led Dot inside. Charlie headed for Bradbury's. I tagged along.

"The wife, I assume?" I said, falling in beside him.

"Yeah, poor cow. Mike leads her a dog's life. You wouldn't believe Dot was as slim as my Julie when she first moved into Buckingham, twelve years ago that was. Her and Mike were already married. She was a lovely looking woman. Mike was always a fat bastard. Chauvinistic doesn't even begin to describe him. Never let Dot work, dinner-on-the-table-when-I-come-home type, not an easy man to get on with."

"I gathered," I said.

"Serves him right getting caught in the storm and having to rough it for a few days at the shop, making his own tea. I'm betting he's gonna be in a foul mood." Charlie laughed.

Reaching the shop, we headed round the back. I pushed the door open when something caught my eye a few yards down the alley. Looking closer, I didn't want to believe what I was seeing.

"Oh fuck..." The words were a whisper.

I turned to Charlie. He was puzzled for a second until I nodded at the bundle of clothes huddled against the wall of the alley. Only they weren't clothes.

"Oh my God."

There was surprisingly little blood. I felt the gorge rise in my throat as Charlie turned away and threw up. Half of Michael's face was missing; only shreds of bloodied flesh hung from his exposed skull. His stomach was an open morass, most of the organs gone. His right arm was nowhere to be seen, and the bones of his right leg gleamed wetly in the sunlight, washed clean by the rain.

"You okay?" I croaked.

"Better than that poor bastard. Jesus, Adam, what happened to him? The storm? An animal?"

"I don't think so, Charlie."

Steeling myself, I looked closer. There were claw marks on the exposed left leg, four straight lines going from groin to knee, straight through the femoral artery. The absence of blood had me wondering; it didn't make sense. I kept seeing the claw marks on my front door, claw marks identical to the ones on Michael's leg.

"I think whatever did this drank his blood," I said.

"Tell me you're joking," Charlie gasped. "You mean like a vampire?"

"No," I grimaced, "lions, leopard, wolves, most predators go for the guts first, opening the victim's stomach, be it man or beast. Whatever did this followed suit, but I think it slashed the femoral artery first to get the blood."

"I don't even want to know how you would know such things." Charlie looked green. "We gotta do something. We can't leave him like this. He needs to be covered, put him somewhere until we can tell someone. If anyone comes round here, kids ..."

"Any suggestions?" I asked. "The shop's no good; people are still liable to go in there, and if Mr. Bradbury should come back, he'd probably have a heart attack."

Charlie thought for a second. "My garage. We can put him there, then go to Wellingham police station and report it. I've got a mate who's a sergeant there; he'll sort this out."

"But we can't move Michael like this. We might be seen."

"Give me a minute; I've got something we can use."

Hurrying down the alley and into my flat, I got a tarpaulin and a hank of paracord from the landing cupboard. I paused, looking at the rope in my hand.

"Paracord, the rope with a thousand uses," I muttered sourly as I headed back to Charlie. *I don't think this was meant to be one of them.*

The paracord reminded me about the line I previously strung across the alley. I remember ducking under it when we cleared the shop. No one could untie my knots, so it stayed where it was. Charlie and I hadn't ducked under the rope when we found Michael.

Charlie was standing with his back to the gruesome corpse, hugging himself. I unrolled the tarp and spread it on the ground beside Michael's remains. It was designed to be waterproof, so it was perfect for the job; the body would be contained.

"Oh God..." Charlie looked away as he helped me roll the body onto the tarp. Slurps and gurgles issued from the cavity of the empty bloody abdomen as we moved him, making our stomachs turn.

I quickly covered Michael as we rolled him over, folding the ends of the tarp closed, tying the ends tight with the paracord like a huge parcel ready for the mail. We stood over the body, pale and expressionless.

"What the hell are we going to tell Dot?" Charlie said in a thick voice.

"The bare minimum, no details," I replied.

Charlie nodded, wiping his mouth. "I'll go get the car before they start to wonder where we are."

Almost as if Charlie had summoned her by voicing his fear, we heard Dot calling his name.

"Charlie, Charlie, you there? Did you find him?"

Charlie threw me a horrified look and hurried out of the alley. I stood on the corner as he intercepted Dot.

"Dot, don't go round there. Michael's not here."

The bereft woman looked at Charlie in confusion. "What d'you mean, not here?"

Julie, followed by several other neighbours, appeared behind Dot.

"Dot, I'm sorry..." Charlie stammered.

He got no further. Dot barged past him and came into the alley. I moved to stop her, but she wasn't going to be stopped.

"Michael! Michael, where are you? You've had me worried…"

Her voice trailed off when she saw the bundle on the ground. Shock registered on her face as realization began to dawn. Her wails began low. Denying the evidence of her eyes, she swayed, her chubby hands cradling her face. She shook her head slowly, the cries of denial rising in her throat before suddenly bursting out in an ear-splitting scream.

Dot rushed forward and dropped by the wrapped bundle, heedless of the glass littering the ground, gashing her knees, not feeling the pain. She began clawing at the tarpaulin, crying and wailing as Charlie and I grabbed her to pull her away. She was strong in her grief, easily pulling out of our combined grip. Getting a hold under her armpits, we dragged her back, kicking and screaming. Julie rushed over and put herself between Dot and the bundle to block her view. Tina helped us get Dot to her feet, blood from her gashed knees flowing down both shins. Tina hugged her and tried to soothe her by telling her, "It's okay. Everything will be okay."

But I knew, for Dot, it would never be okay again.

Dot's huge frame heaved up as she fought to take breath, her wails faded, and her tear-stained face, pale as cottage cheese, went blank as she stared into nothingness. She looked around the gathered people as if searching for something until her eyes fell on me.

"This is your fault," she spoke in a whisper, but everyone could hear. "If you hadn't stopped him taking the chocolate in the first place, he wouldn't have come back for it. You had no right! NO RIGHT! This is all your doing!"

"Dot, shush, shush, it's no one's fault. No one could have known this was going to happen," Tina soothed.

"He should have let Michael have the chocolate. There was no harm in it; it was only chocolate…"

Her words hit me like a sledgehammer. She was right. If I hadn't stopped him… I looked down at the parcel at my feet. In my mind's eye, I could see the mutilated body beneath. A man had died all because of a few bars of chocolate.

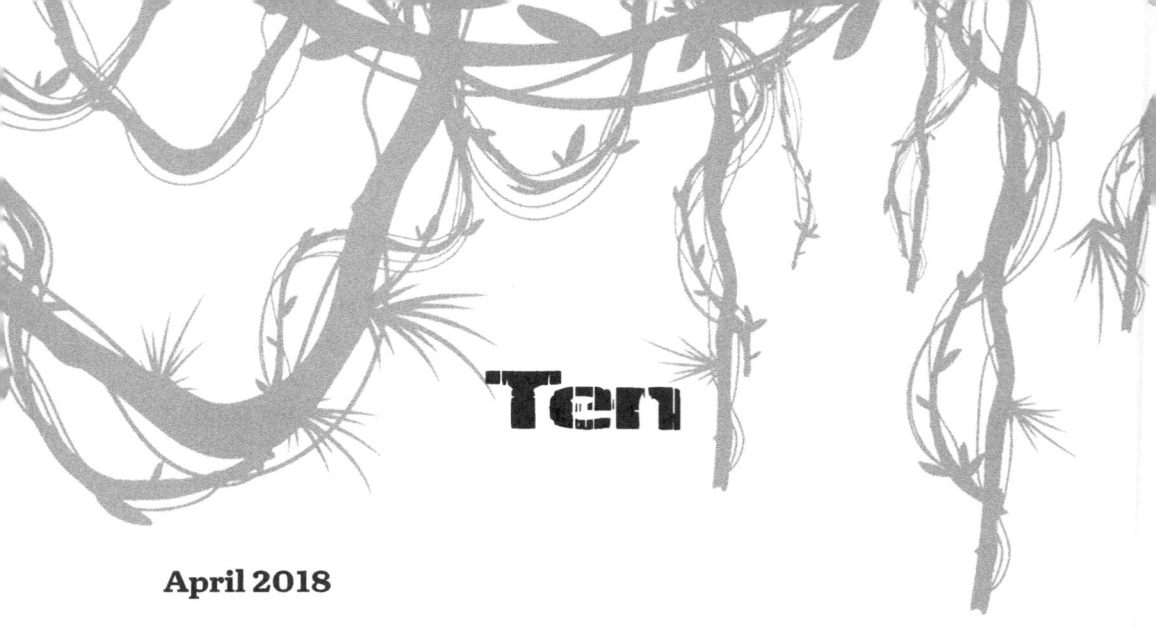

Ten

April 2018

"She didn't mean it," Charlie said as we turned onto Yorkland Road. "She was in shock, upset."

"Because I'd just got her husband killed," I said bleakly, watching the streets go by.

"Then I'm as much to blame as you are. I was there," Charlie said.

"Maybe," I said tiredly. I'd had enough of talking.

I suddenly remembered why I liked to be alone. Interaction with people always seemed to bring me grief, even with the best of intentions.

Julie and Tina had finally managed to get Dot back into the house while Charlie and I moved Michael's body to the garage. Not the most auspicious of resting places, but it was the best we could manage. Now we had to inform the authorities of his death, which was why we were headed for the Wellingham police station. What they would make of it was anyone's guess. Whilst Julie and Tina had attended to Dot in the alley, I checked on the paracord I had strung across it. It had been cut. Strangely, the cord didn't meet, and about four inches was missing as if it had been cut in two places. *Why would someone do that? Maybe it hadn't been cut; maybe it had been bitten.*

Wellingham looked washed out. There was black Dust residue everywhere, and people still had shocked and bewildered expressions as they ventured out.

"Just how widespread do you think the deluge was?" Charlie asked as we turned onto Cumberland Avenue.

"Evidently, it covered all of Wellingham," I said.

"It can't have just been us," he replied. "We wouldn't have lost the T.V. or mobile phone service if it had just been local."

"Maybe your policeman friend will be able to shed some light on the subject, give us some answers."

"You think so?" Charlie said sceptically.

"No," I said.

Reaching the end of Hook Lane, we turned onto the high street. It was like a ghost town, nothing was open, and all the shops were shuttered and dark. Here and there, people were looking through glass shop fronts, hands cupping their faces against the windows hopefully. They came away disappointed.

"I guess it was too much to hope for," Charlie said glumly.

"They need time," I said. "First the dust, then the rain, its freaked people out. They need time to recover, get things back to normal."

The trees lining the roads we traversed had ivy entwined at the base of their trunks. Many of the front lawns of the semi-detached houses were overgrown. The grass in some of them was well over a foot tall, as were the hedges separating the gardens, some spilling out over the pavements. It was odd, but I didn't really take that much notice; I already had too much on my mind to worry about overgrown gardens.

At the police station, Charlie parked the car and I followed him inside. The reception area was buzzing with at least two dozen people, men and women clamouring for attention.

"I didn't expect this," Charlie muttered.

There was no way we would be served any time soon. The officer attending the desk was already harried, and despite his best attempts, Charlie couldn't get himself noticed.

"We'll have to wait," I said. "We haven't got much option."

"Wait a minute. Stay here," Charlie said, pushing his way through the crowd towards a policeman who had just

entered the reception area from outside. They exchanged a few words, then Charlie struggled his way back to me.

"Let's get outside," he said, being jostled. "Colin's gonna meet us there."

Never being one for crowds, it was a relief to get into the open again. I also recognised the familiar signs: irritation nagged at me more and more easily the last few days. No one's fault, just a personality trait quietly informing me that it was time to get away. I pushed the thought out of my mind as I looked up and down the near deserted high street.

Outside the police station, a decorative cannon set on a small grassy knoll close to the corner was covered in ivy, entwining the wheels and making its way along the bronze muzzle; grass nearly reached the gun's underbelly. Outside the library, two flowerpots, huge concrete affairs, were also overgrown, vines trailing to the pavement, gently blown by the breeze. Then I realised there was no breeze.

"Charlie, good to see you! You come to make a complaint as well?"

Distracted, I turned as a tall, uniformed man exited a side door to the police station. He was a typical policeman: tall, short dark hair, clean shaven. He took Charlie's proffered hand and shook it warmly.

"I wish," Charlie said bleakly. "Colin Pearson, Adam Blake," he said by way of introduction.

"Nice to meet you, Adam," he said, shaking my hand. "Now, what can I do for you?"

Charlie told him, leaving nothing out.

"And you think a dog was responsible?" Pearson asked when Charlie had finished.

"A big dog," Charlie emphasised. "Jesus, you should have seen it; his bloody arm was missing."

The policeman looked at us both as if weighing something up in his mind. "I shouldn't be telling you this," he began. "This isn't the first of these attacks that has been reported. In fact, yours is the seventh."

"Seven? Around here?" I asked, shocked.

"No, two in Eltham, three in Dartford, and one in Erith. And now Wellingham," Colin said.

"That can't be just one dog," I said. "The locations are too far apart. Eltham to Erith has got to be six miles."

"The total area is fifteen square miles," Colin agreed. "I checked."

"You saying there's a pack of killer dogs out there somewhere?" Charlie asked.

"We don't know for sure," Colin said. "We're not even sure it's dogs."

"The claw marks," I said.

"Exactly," said Colin. "How did you know?"

I felt a little uncomfortable. "You remember that first day, when I got the food to you?" I asked Charlie.

He nodded.

"On the way to your place, going through the dust, something brushed against me. I thought it was just some rubbish and didn't take any notice. After I left you, the line guiding me back to my place was cut. If not for Linda, I would have been lost. Later that night we heard something at the front door. We investigated..."

Charlie looked at me, his face going pale, as I told them about the eyes and the claw marks.

"You mean you knew about these ... these animals and said nothing?" he asked in a low whisper. "Jesus, Adam, there's kids on the street, my kids."

"I didn't know then what we know now. I thought it was just a dog driven crazy by the dust."

"Holy shit," Charlie said. "We need to tell the others back on Buckingham Avenue, get people off the street."

"I think you should," Pearson said. "I'll make arrangements for your friend; there'll have to be an autopsy. Keep close to home until we can bring some order to the situation."

"What about communications? Mobile phones? When are we going to get them back?" I asked.

"I've no information when, or even *if,* services will be restored. It's a catch twenty-two situation."

"What about police radios?" asked Charlie.

"Out of commission. It's a total black out," said Colin.

"Shit," Charlie replied.

Charlie drove a lot faster back than he did getting here, his knuckles white on the steering wheel.

"It's okay, Charlie. Don't worry. They'll be safe," I said.

He shot me a glance. Anger, partnered with fear, danced in his eyes. "Tell that to Michael," he said testily.

We drove in silence for a while. Charlie visibly relaxed when Buckingham Avenue came into view.

"It's like the whole fucking world's gone to shit," he murmured.

"We'll figure it out, Charlie. Find out what's going on and put it to rights," I said.

Charlie looked very subdued as he parked outside his house. Not wanting to intrude, I headed home, plus the feeling of wanting to get away was getting stronger by the minute.

I had no appetite. The T.V. was still out, so I put some music on the CD player and threw myself onto the couch. I didn't want to think of anything. I just concentrated on listening to Passenger sing his doleful songs.

I must have drifted off because the next thing I knew it was mid-afternoon and the electricity supply was out. I checked the street and couldn't see any lights anywhere. It was too much. I gave up and sat on the bottom step of the stairs with my head in my hands.

"Fuck" was all I had the strength to say.

How long I sat there is anyone's guess. It might have only been minutes; I don't know. A shadow filled the open front door.

"It's not getting any better, is it?" Tina said.

I tried to smile and failed miserably.

"If it's any consolation, we still have water," she said brightly.

"Small blessings," I agreed.

"Come on, we're firing up the B.B.Q. Everyone's meeting at mine. You're invited, but you bring the sausages," Tina said.

Maybe the tiredness was brought on by too many beers; I don't know. I remember grabbing some sausages and a pack of beef burgers from the freezer, they were already defrosting, and went over to Tina's. That's about all I remember.

Charlie was still subdued and wasn't talking. Neither was Julie, who had spent a hard few hours trying to console the inconsolable Dot. With the help of a couple of sleeping pills, Dot slept on the sofa in their front room. I vaguely remembered something about Tina's back garden, which like most of the gardens in the area was paved since it was too small to warrant lawns or elaborate flowerbeds. Brightly coloured flowerpots filled Tina's garden, a reflection of her character. I also noticed they were overgrown...

Drinking whilst depressed is not a good idea as the following morning testified. I'd no idea how I got to my bed. I'm guessing with a drunk's unerring sense of direction. The room was dark even though I didn't remember drawing the curtains. I flipped on the bedside lamp.

"Bollocks," I said softly when the room remained in darkness.

I sat on the bed, my mouth as dry as the Sahara, a dull thudding at the back of my head.

"Double bollocks," I said again.

The day was spent alone. I'm guessing Charlie and my neighbours were in the same frame of mind as I received no visitors, thankfully. It gave me time to check over my camping gear. No decision had crystalized in my mind just yet, but on some level, I knew I was going to get away, maybe Wales, maybe Scotland, definitely remote. Tent, sleeping bag, and the remaining tarp were all stacked at the foot of the stairs by the front door along with my cook set, sadly depleted paracord and utensils. I hadn't meant to go camping; I'd actually got my camping stove out of storage in case the gas went out, and it just went on from there.

It calmed me, had me looking forward to being out in the wild, alone in peace. I think that's the only time I was truly at peace. Sitting by a campfire in Cairngorm Forest or in the Lakes, drinking coffee or maybe a beer, watching the stars, listening to the night sounds. I could almost smell the breakfast bacon, hear it sizzling in the pan over the fire with an egg or two whilst admiring the view in front of my tent, the Scottish Highlands around Applecross or one of the lochs, Doon maybe or Maree. I knew of a great spot on the shores of Loch Maree where I could spend a few days. It would be like coming home.

The knock at the door broke my reverie. With a sigh, I went and answered it.

"Charlie?" I said in surprise.

He looked defeated. I guess I wasn't the only one feeling the strain of the last week.

"Hi, mate," he said. "Julie sent me over, thought you might want dinner. I don't think she likes the idea of you being alone."

"Cheers, Charlie, but not tonight. I'm bushed and just want a little time alone."

"I figured you would, but Julie wanted to make sure. Oh, FYI, I've let people know about the animal attacks, told 'em there was nothing to worry about, just a few dogs and that the police had it under control. I think it did the trick."

"Thanks, Charlie," I said.

"No prob. See you in the morning."

As he turned to go, Charlie spotted my camping gear behind me and frowned.

"You going somewhere?" he asked.

I looked at the gear. For some reason, I suddenly felt guilty.

"Thinking about it," I answered as casually as I could.

"Really?" I could hear the accusation in his voice. "In the middle of all this, the storms, Michael?"

"Charlie..." I didn't have the words.

"No, mate, it's all right. You go. The rest of us will manage. Jesus! What happened to us all pulling together, help each other, isn't that what you said?"

"It's all but over," I countered. "The electricity will be back on soon, the storms have passed, and now it's in the hands of the authorities. I'm not needed for that."

"No, course not. Never mind about Michael or the families still struggling to cope; they're not your responsibility. Or the animals still running loose killing people!"

"Your friend, the policeman, already told you that's under control."

"I thought you were my friend," Charlie cut in.

"Charlie, I am."

"Yeah, course you are. Forget it. You go on your little camping trip. You don't owe anyone anything."

He turned and stomped off, leaving me standing on the doorstep. The words stuck in my throat; I just didn't know what to say.

"Well, that went well," I muttered angrily as I closed the door.

Sleep didn't come easily that night. Maybe that's why I overslept. I intended to leave early, get the cab from storage and just go. Laying in the dark thinking about Charlie and Dot, I wish we hadn't argued. I kept telling myself Charlie was right, even though he said it in anger. I wasn't responsible for them. The crisis was over, and now was the time to gain control of our lives again. The authorities would move in and take the reins. I had every right to get away if I wanted to. The electricity was out, so there was no point going back to work just yet. I deserved a break. Yeah, right. *So why do I feel like a shit running away?*

After some Weetabix for breakfast and a quick, cold shower, I went to get the cab. The day was a little overcast, but it was warm enough. The storage parking lot was only a ten-minute walk, and I wasn't surprised to find it unmanned. It was good to get behind the wheel again, especially as there wasn't much traffic on the road. It gave me time to think.

Wellingham was still reeling, trying to redress situations unprecedented in their experience. Shit, it was unprecedented in everyone's experience. I drove around for a while to clear my head. With all the services out and the shops temporarily closed, it would only be a matter of time before bewilderment turned to anger and people would start to demand action, not to mention answers. I couldn't blame them; I just didn't want to be around when the arguments started. Scotland was looking more attractive by the minute.

As I drove, I was drawn to the sides of the roadway. Kent County took great care of their motorways, manicured verges, cultured bushes and shrubs, well-trimmed trees. It held the distinction of being "The Garden of England."

"Highway maintenance is going to have its hands full when they see this lot," I murmured, looking at the long grasses invading the hard-shoulder, unkempt bushes, and vine-ladened trees.

Taking the Blackfen turn-off, I headed for home. There was a lot of activity as I pulled onto the roundabout at the bottom of the road, so I pulled over. Several adults had formed a perimeter circling the roundabout which incredibly boasted at least five feet of growth, encompassing the entire knoll.

"Jesus..."

Closer inspection showed the strange ivy-like plant I had seen all over Wellingham, only now I could see it was no variety of ivy I had ever seen. The vines were a purple-black colour with livid green leaves; vicious looking thorns covered the growth, slim, white and glistening.

"What's going on?"

One of the men surrounding the roundabout glanced my way. I think I knew him from the shop rationing, but his name escaped me for the moment.

"The Baxter girl got stung by one of the vines. Her parents rushed her to hospital. She collapsed, out cold."

"Collapsed?"

"Yeah, she said the vine waved at her. When she went nearer, it grabbed her around the arm. The thorns are secreting some sort of poison. And then she just fainted."

It didn't seem credible, but after the events of the last week, who was I to judge? I moved closer to the undergrowth, and it rustled and whispered. Suddenly, someone grabbed me from behind and pulled me back just as one of the vines lashed out, missing my face by inches. The whole roundabout exploded into movement as vines thrashed and whipped through the air. Thankfully, their range was limited and couldn't reach me. They continued to writhe like purple-black snakes, their rustling echoing the serpentine hiss.

"Fuck," I said, turning to my benefactor. I should have known it was Charlie.

"Close call, mate. They're bloody lethal."

We scrambled to our feet.

"I, for one, have had enough of this shit!" Charlie said as he filled a glass bottle with petrol from a can at his feet. "It's about time we became proactive and did something."

He pulled a piece of rag from his waistband and stuffed it tightly into the neck of the petrol filled bottle.

"Stay back everyone!" he yelled as he lit the rag with a lighter.

"Charlie, it won't work!" I shouted.

"We'll see about that!" he said and lobbed the bottle into the middle of the writhing plants.

Several people turned their faces away as the flaming Molotov cocktail arched through the air. They tensed, waiting for the burst of flame, and then … nothing.

Charlie's look of surprise would have been comical if the situation hadn't been so serious.

"The ground's too soft Charlie; the bottle can't break!" I said.

Anger and frustration darkened his face. "So, what do we do?" he growled.

I thought for a second. "Balloons, plastic bags, anything that can hold liquid but tear easily," I said.

"Freezer bags?" Charlie said.

"Anything," I answered.

He rushed off and came back a few minutes later carrying a blue plastic bucket with the black bin bags we had used to bag up the Dust.

"Not enough freezer bags but I've got these," he said, holding up a blue and red box.

"Perfect, if a little big," I said.

Charlie grinned and produced a pair of large scissors. I shook my head in wonder.

Cutting the bags down and placing them in the bucket, we filled them with petrol.

"Just twist them shut. The vines own thorns will do the job of splitting them for us," I said.

Within minutes, we had a dozen bags sitting in a pile in the road.

"Right, everyone grab a bag, careful now. Surround the bushes and throw them in. Try and spread them as far apart as we can, not all in the middle."

The men took the bags, getting into position around the writhing island.

"Okay, now!" I shouted.

The bags flew, and it was satisfying to see them rip and tear on the lashing thorns, spilling the amber liquid, saturating the roundabout.

"Now you do the honours, Charlie," I said.

Charlie soaked another rag in petrol and jammed it into an empty bottle, leaving a length dangling. With a grim smile, he used his lighter. The rag flared and Charlie let rip. This time, there was a *whump* as the petrol caught. A massive sheet of flame reached up into the sky, enveloping the entire roundabout. The vines writhed and thrashed frantically as fire tore into them, leaves withered, thorns curled, branches blazed. Cheers of triumph erupted from the gathered crowd as the deadly plants burned. The heat drove us back as we watched. Half an hour later, there was nothing left but ash.

Eleven

April 2018

Our jubilation was short lived. A few hours later, the Baxters returned from the hospital, pale, shaken, in deep shock. Melissa, their daughter, had died. There was nothing the doctors could do. The poison in Melissa's system was unidentifiable, and they couldn't prevent it from systematically shutting down all her bodily functions. David Baxter told us these things in a stunned whisper as if speaking it aloud would make it a reality. Tears flowed down his gaunt face until he was unable to speak any more. He and his wife shuffled off towards an empty home, locked in each other's arms.

People burned their gardens, flowerpots, window boxes, any piece of greenery that was spawning the horror that had killed a child. Charlie used the last of the petrol on his and Tina's back gardens. Others used whatever flammables they had from B.B.Q. lighter fluid to cigarette lighter refills. One guy destroyed the plants outside the Falcon Pub using an old type blow torch intended for stripping paint. They set about the task with a grim sort of glee, in their minds exacting revenge for Melissa Baxter.

It carried on into the evening, the smell of burning acrid on the air. I was quietly glad that it gave them all a sense of achievement, if only a little, a sense that they had struck back at the misfortunes that had beset them over the last two weeks. They gathered by the roundabout, a sort of subdued euphoria settling over them. Some of them hugged; others just said their goodnights as they all drifted off to their respective homes.

"Hey," Charlie said as we stood side by side, watching our neighbours disperse into the dusk. "Look, about last night, I'm sorry. I..."

"It's okay, Charlie. It's been a bad few days for all of us."

"Yeah," he said and fell quiet.

"Hey, you two!" Julie called. "Which one of you is firing up the B.B.Q. tonight? We're getting hungry!"

"Yeah!" piped up David, clutching his mother's hand.

I frowned, "B.B.Q. again?"

"No choice, mate," Charlie said. "Our stove's electric, can't live on cold baked beans."

"Shit, Charlie, why didn't you say something? Get the kids. We're eating at mine," I said. "No arguments."

Good old bangers and mash, peas, and onion gravy. Magic! Beer for us, Coke for the kids, a glass of white wine for Julie, and a feast fit for a king. After we'd eaten and cleared everything away, we sat in the living room quietly enjoying each other's company by candlelight.

"You're looking serious again," Julie remarked, leaning against Charlie on the sofa. The kids were on the floor reading some of my old superhero magazines.

"Just thinking about today," I said, looking at the kids and trying to keep my voice low. "I'm not sure people appreciate the ramifications of what happened with the vines."

"What d'you mean?" Charlie asked.

"When we went to Wellingham, I noticed a lot of the gardens were overgrown, several trees had vines entwined around their trunks. I thought it was ivy, but now I'm not so sure."

"Vines? Like those on the roundabout?" Charlie said, leaning forward.

"I don't know. To be honest, I didn't really look. I tend to notice things like that, things out of the ordinary. There was more on the A2; I saw them when I picked up the cab."

"Bloody hell. Maybe we should check, have a closer look," Charlie suggested.

"Is that safe?" Julie asked, also sitting up, her wine forgotten in her hand.

"We need to know, love," Charlie said.

"You're still not getting it, Charlie," I said. "Wellingham is surrounded by countryside, parks, woods, most of the urban towns are. What if the vines are there growing unimpeded? We need to go back to Colin, tell him what happened here today. People need to know the vines are dangerous."

"That's gonna be a mission with no communications. How do we let people know?"

"We'll have to rely on word of mouth, make sure people understand. Maybe Colin can arrange for cars equipped with loudspeakers to cruise the area."

"It's a damn shame losing the electricity. We could have used computers to print off warning flyers, post them everywhere, put them through people's letterboxes."

"We could still do that. We can make the flyers by hand, nothing complicated, just clearly written warnings," Julie said.

"Maybe we can get some of the neighbours involved, give the kids something constructive to do?" Charlie said.

"I'll talk to them in the morning. I'm sure Tina will help."

"Wait, listen..." I said.

The room fell silent. A faint cracking could be heard. Going to the window, I opened it and leaned out. The discordant cracking sound was clearer.

"Who the hell would be setting off fireworks?" Charlie said beside me. "What's there to celebrate?"

I listened for a few seconds longer.

"That's not fireworks," I said. "That's gunfire."

The sun had not yet risen as I towelled myself dry. A cold, pre-dawn shower by candlelight, *life couldn't get any better, could it?* I smiled thinly. Hearing the gunfire put a premature end to yesterday evening. Charlie and Julie bundled the kids home. A bad end to a bad day.

The gunfire had worried me too; it brought Linda to mind. She said she would come back and let me know everything was all right. Last night's gunfire came from the direction of Denford Park, and Stack Road ran parallel to the park. Visions of the vines haunted me; the one that lashed out at me missed by inches. If not for Charlie... I couldn't get it out of my mind.

A thin, white line cracked the eastern horizon as dawn broke. With it came the roar of engines from outside. Grabbing my jacket, I went downstairs.

"What the...?"

An army personnel carrier was crawling along Buckingham Avenue, two squads of armed soldiers on either side keeping pace. Other soldiers, equally armed, were banging on people's doors yelling for them to wake up.

"Hey, mate, what's going on? What's all the noise about?"

"Evacuation," came the curt reply. "You need to gather some belongings and move to a designated safe area immediately," the soldier said.

"Safe area? What are you talking about? What safe area? Why?"

"A state of emergency has been declared. The entire area is being evacuated to designated safe areas, Queen Elizabeth Hospital, Greenwich Hospital, Queen Mary's Hospital. It's for your own safety. You need to comply immediately."

"You still haven't said why," I pointed out, already knowing I wasn't going to get an answer.

"I don't have that information, Sir. You just need to comply."

The soldier sounded like a broken record.

"Has this anything to do with the gunfire I heard last night?" I asked.

"I don't have that information, Sir. Please comply. Get whatever you need and go to the nearest safe area."

The street was filling up as people came out in response to the ruckus. Many were alarmed to find armed soldiers banging on their doors at the crack of dawn. I saw Tina across the road animatedly talking to Charlie and Julie. Charlie saw me and hurried over.

"What the fuck is going on now?" he said, anger edging his voice.

"I think it's got something to do with the gunfire we heard last night, not that anyone's actually saying that. A soldier told me a state of emergency has been declared but not why."

"You think it's the vines?" Charlie asked.

"They wouldn't be shooting vines, Charlie. This is something else," I answered. "You better do as they ask. Get Julie and the kids to Queen Elizabeth's Hospital. Tina as well if you've got the room. I'll meet you there."

"And where are you going?" he asked.

I told him about Linda. "It's probably nothing, but I need to check."

"Dunno if the soldier boys will allow that," Charlie said dubiously.

"I won't be asking them," I said with a wink. "I'll see you later; keep safe."

I went back upstairs and shoved a few things in a backpack. Hesitating briefly, I took down my rifle and some spare ammunition from the top of the wardrobe and put it all into the cab. The camping gear went into the boot. The future was suddenly looking very uncertain, and I figured to cover as many eventualities as possible.

Locking up, I got into the cab. The street was a hive of activity. People were complaining as they loaded their cars, kids were bundled into back seats, hastily packed suitcases and bags thrown into the boot. All the while, vigilant soldiers made sure everything was going as fast and as smoothly as possible.

Eyes were on me, waiting to see what I was doing. I waved at a couple of the soldiers and slowly pulled away from the kerb. A couple of cars pulled out behind me, Charlie's Focus among them. I waited until I was level with the rear access running behind the houses, then turned left and drove quickly into the alley, hoping to bypass the cordon before they realised what I was doing.

No such luck. There was a patrol, three soldiers, about halfway down the alley coming towards me; one of them raised his hand and ordered me to stop. Slowing as if complying, I dipped the clutch, and the cab kept rolling. Thirty yards from the men, I gunned the engine, popped the clutch, and sped forward, giving the surprised soldiers ample time to get out of the way as I barrelled through. They shouted and waved but made no attempt to unsling their automatic weapons. I smiled grimly, thankful for small mercies as I came out of the alley. Looking left and right, another personnel carrier was to my left, so I turned right, tearing up

Buckingham Avenue to Northumberland. I turned right again and found myself in the clear.

In every street there were squads of soldiers, jeeps and personnel carriers pushing Wellingham's inhabitants continually north towards Queen Elizabeth Hospital, about four miles away just before Greenwich. It was easy enough to avoid them, even though my route became a little circuitous. The evacuation was well prepared, which made me wonder exactly what the "state of emergency" was. With a growing sense of foreboding, I knew it wouldn't be anything good.

Reaching Stack Road, I realised a little flaw in my plan to find Linda; I didn't know her house number.

"Brilliant," I muttered, looking down a very long road of semi-detached houses.

A Mini. She said she had a Mini and that it had broken down outside the house. Empty house, Mini parked outside—how hard could it be to locate? Unless she'd got the Mini fixed, of course.

The smell of burning was in the air. Not the sweet smell of B.B.Q. or burning leaves. This was a bitter assault on the sinuses. Vast patches of scorched earth fronted many of the houses; the lower trunks of the horse chestnut trees lining the road were singed enough to destroy the vines and cause minimal damage to the tree. People were alerted to the danger of the thorns, but I hoped the cost of discovery hadn't been too high.

The road was deserted; the people already evacuated. There were still a few cars parked in front of some of the houses. I guessed second family cars, surplus to requirements. The blue Mini was covered in Dustin the driveway, normal Dust acquired from standing idle for a few days. The house looked unoccupied with no curtains or blinds up at the windows. I knocked on the door, not really expecting an answer. I wasn't disappointed.

Looking through the windows showed me nothing but empty rooms. This had to be Linda's house, but I wanted to be a hundred percent certain. The side gate leading to the rear of the house had no lock, so I went through. Stopping in my tracks, I stared at the cluster of vines writhing on the narrow path at the corner of the house. A low rustling

filled the air as a vine wavered above the bush lethargically, sunlight glistening on the wicked, white thorns.

"Bollocks," I cursed, retreating the way I had come and closing the gate behind me.

Throwing caution to the wind, I smashed one of the windows in the front door with my elbow. Reaching in, I threw the lock and opened the door.

"Linda! Linda, are you here?"

The rooms remained silent. The interior of the house was stuffy, airless. The place hadn't been aired in some time. Making a hurried search of the rooms, I confirmed the house was empty. Doubt still nagged at me. I wanted to know for certain. The red scarf lay in the corner, lost in shadow. I snatched it up and recognised the perfume; it was Linda's. *So, she had been here, but where was she now? Had her husband made it back? Had they been evacuated together?* But that would mean the evacuation wasn't new. It must have started some days ago, maybe longer.

I was becoming more and more aware that there was more to recent events than I knew. I was beginning to think the authorities had more information than they were telling. Colin Pearson knew more than he let on when we met him.

Curiosity piqued, I headed back.

Twelve

April 2018

Lines of vehicles were heading for the A2 Motorway: cars, vans, even a truck or two. Anger, fear, confusion reflected on the faces of all the occupants. The world had gone mad, and they couldn't get to grips with it. They were running, but I wondered how many of them actually knew what they were running from or where they were running to.

Thankfully, I was going in the opposite direction, so my way was unimpeded until I got to the Whitehouse Roundabout at the junction of Bexley Road and Denford Road.

"Sorry, Cabbie. Can't come through here. State of emergency," the army sergeant informed me when I stopped in front of the barrier blocking Denford Road.

"You've got to be kidding me?" I said in my best exasperated tone. "I live in Park Vista Road. How am I s'posed to get home?"

"Sorry, everyone's being evacuated. Roads are closing," the sergeant explained.

"Evacuated? Closed? What for? What's going on?"

"All I can tell you is a state of emergency has been called, and we have orders to evacuate the area of all civilians."

I had to give it to the military; they were consistent in their non-disclosure policy, and everybody was reading from the same script.

"Look, mate, with all that's been going on, I need to earn a living. I've been out all night and got sod all to show for it. I'm tired, I'm hungry, and I just want to get home. I'll shower, change me clothes, and have something to eat, then I'll evacuate to wherever you want me to. Come on. Give me a break."

The sergeant hesitated, and I could see he empathised with me. I've no idea why, but I wasn't going to let the opportunity pass.

"An hour, ninety minutes at most, honest," I urged.

"You go straight home. Do not enter the park. Do what you have to do, and then go straight to a designated safe area, in your case, Queen Elizabeth Hospital." He looked at me gravely before continuing, "My brother-in-law's a cabbie. All this trouble has caused him and my sister no end of money problems. I'm trusting you, cabbie."

I felt a twinge of guilt as he ordered his men to remove the barrier.

"Cheers, mate. You're a diamond."

I drove through.

Denford Road was swarming with military and police vehicles. There were several in the park to my left, head-lights glaring even though it was still daylight, blue, red and amber lights flashing. Then, I realised that I shouldn't have been able to see them or the park's wrought iron perimeter gates which were usually obscured by a wall of dense foliage. Towards the centre of the park was Denford Lake; in happier times, people went boating or fishing or just admired the view. Beyond the lake, bright flashes caught my eye. It was difficult to look as the road ahead was busy. A military jeep decided to U-turn, affording me a few seconds to see what was happening across the far side of the lake.

Flamethrowers. They're using flamethrowers.

The road was clear and I carried on. The thoughts I had earlier about parks, woodlands, and countryside being overrun echoed in my mind.

Oh, sweet Jesus.

The park gates appeared on the left, huge, black wrought iron affairs opening onto a two-lane tarmac road that led straight down to the boathouse. Smaller paths branched off the main road for walkers and their pets, no vehicles allowed. Paths led around the lake, others to the woods, and one went over the stone bridge that crossed the lake.

Army vehicles, like squatting green beetles in shadow of the gates, were lined up in a row just outside of the opening. A gap in the line afforded me a parking space. Feeling somewhat conspicuous in a white cab amongst all the green, I turned off the engine and got out. No one took any notice of me as I stood by the cab, presuming I had legitimate business. Just on the other side of the park gates, several green canvas tents had been erected. Uniformed men, both military and police, frequently came and went. There was extensive evidence of burning. There wasn't a tree or bush within fifty yards of the small conclave.

A sudden burst of gunfire from the wooded area on the east side of the park startled me. Sporadic bursts followed then fell silent. *Guns against plants? What the fuck is going on?*

Exiting one of the tents, an army officer barked some orders at a sergeant who quickly bellowed for his men to fall in. Within seconds, the squad formed and was led off by the officer towards the woods. The area suddenly felt deserted. Two armed soldiers stood either side of the gate, another by the line of jeeps, and three policemen were near the entrance to the largest of the tents. It was a little disconcerting to see police officers armed with pistols holstered at their waists.

Then Colin Pearson stepped out of the tent and spoke to the policemen.

"Sergeant Pearson," I said, standing between the two soldiers at the gate.

The policeman turned and was unable to disguise the look of surprise when he saw me. He said something to one of the policemen before walking over to me. Pearson shook my hand as if we were out for a Sunday stroll or something.

"Adam, isn't it?" he asked disarmingly.

"Yeah," I replied. "Adam Blake, Charlie's friend."

"Yes, of course. I should be asking you what you are doing in a secure area, Mr. Blake, and how you managed to get past the barricade?"

"I lied," I said bluntly.

He barely suppressed the smile. "I admire your candour."

"Then do me a favour and return it," I said, "and tell me what's going on here?"

I saw that same steely look he gave me outside the police station.

"You knew something was wrong before me and Charlie spoke to you, didn't you? You knew about the vines," I prompted.

"No," he said slowly, "not exactly."

"But you knew they were dangerous," I pushed.

"We knew there was some danger, just not how much. We only learned they were lethal after we had spoken."

"A young girl died because of those vines—poisoned. It could have been prevented," I said.

"Melissa Baxter. Yes, I know," he said. "And I'm truly sorry. She was one of several casualties before the true danger was discovered."

"She might not have been a casualty if you had said something, given us a warning," I said harshly.

Pearson visibly winced. "It may be of little consolation, but I wish I had. In my defence, all I can offer is that I wasn't made fully aware of the danger."

I had no answer to this. He seemed sincere, genuine. I changed the subject. "Why are they using guns against plants?" I asked.

"Ah," he said, "walk with me."

Walking through the gates, we made our way between the tents where we came across two rows of bulky, black rubber sacks laid out on the ground. One row was considerably longer than the other. With horror, I realised what they were.

"I'm sorry. I didn't mean to shock you," Pearson said. "I just wanted you to know I did take you seriously when we spoke, more serious than you could know. And to answer your question, we're not using guns against the vines. Rather, we're using them on your 'wild dogs,' only they're not dogs.

"Unfortunately, it was another instance of poor intel. We lost several men before we realised the new danger. Despite killing them in great numbers, we are still vastly outnumbered. Go on. See for yourself; they're not very big, but they're ugly brutes and extremely efficient killing machines. I'd say you were very lucky in your encounter with them. Others were not so fortunate."

I didn't want to look but felt an odd fascination. Kneeling by the first bag, I reached for the zipper, surprised to find my hand was shaking. Taking a deep breath, I pulled the zipper down and came face to face with a pair of lifeless red and black eyes set in a monstrous face. The head was almost an inverted oval, hairless except for a tuft of white coarse hair running through the centre of the skull like a punk's Mohawk. Its face was flat with no nose to speak of, just two slits for nostrils. The mouth was small, full of sharp teeth, jagged, sharp. Its bright red tongue lolled from its maw like a grotesque scarlet slug.

"It's got white fur over its shoulders, belly, and legs, but reptilian scales down its sides, back, and neck; the skin is a mottled grey, no tail, standing between three and four feet tall. It's ape-like, but the scales indicate a reptile's genes. It also has four fingers with opposable thumbs. The men call them 'Creeps' because they are fast and silent and don't seem to vocalise, not even a grunt, which also begs the question: How do they communicate with each other?"

"Christ," I said, wrinkling my nose.

"Oh, and they stink," added Pearson.

"Where did they come from?" I asked, rezipping the bag, relieved at putting the dead thing out of sight.

"No real idea, though it's obvious that the black dust, the vines, and these brutes are all connected somehow." Pearson indicated we should leave the area. "It's conceivable that the vines came down in seed form with the dust. How the Creeps manifested themselves is a mystery."

I looked around as we came out from between the tents. There was a lot of manpower here, ordinance, and vehicles. I voiced a question that had been bugging me.

"How is it that a police sergeant is in charge of such an operation?"

Pearson smiled grimly. "Not through choice," he said, a cloud passing over his face. "My superior, Chief Inspector Munroe, should be in command. Unfortunately, he was one of the first casualties here in the park as he was walking his dog. He and the dog were badly mutilated. The odd thing was, though his wounds were severe, they were smaller than recent evidence."

"Indicating a young animal," I suggested.

"Exactly. Which means the Creeps were somehow born here. There's been some wild theories amongst our tech guys. One even suggested they came down as embryos, that they may even be parthenogenic."

He saw my puzzled expression.

"It means they can self-produce young without sex."

We stopped in front of the tents. It was not long past noon. I was feeling somewhat surreal, walking in a burnt park talking about monsters that self-produce with a policeman. Gunfire chattered to the east.

"Why are you telling me all this?" I asked. "Doesn't it contravene the Official Secrets Act or something?"

Pearson's smile was bitter. "I think we are way past that. I've got a strong feeling that this whole situation is going to escalate beyond the boundaries of the police and all the armed forces to contain. The people need to know what's going on. They need to try and defend themselves as best they can, but there's no way to tell them except by word of mouth. You, and people like you, can help to get that particular ball rolling."

He continued, "The black Dust caused some sort of E.M.P. effect, fried everything electronic. I'm told a new communications system is being developed, but I have no time frame. I believe the effect is dissipating since the black Dust stopped falling; the static on our radios is getting less and less. I'm hoping it will clear all together, but until then, word of mouth is all we've got."

"To paraphrase Charlie, it's a bloody nightmare," I muttered, looking out over the parkland.

Superficially, it was a beautiful day, clear sky, warm breeze, and then I smelled the cordite in the air, burning wood, heard the chatter of gunfire. The illusion shattered.

"You had better get to a safe zone," Pearson said. "Maybe you can organise some sort of general meeting, let people know what you have learned here."

"Sir! There's movement on the tree line!" called one of the policemen, pointing to the trees to the north about sixty yards away.

"Did you see what it was?" Pearson asked, scanning the trees.

"No sir, just a lot of movement in the lower branches," the policeman said.

"Keep your eyes open. Be alert. We need to be prepared for anything."

Those words would stick in my mind for a long time because we weren't prepared for what happened next. Suddenly, the soldier by the line of jeeps gagged, a scream stifled in his throat. Aghast, I watched as a Creep clung to his chest, razor sharp claws raking his face and neck. A second Creep hung on his back, teeth gnashing. Blood flew as the struggling bodies fell out of sight behind the vehicles.

The policeman who had given the warning drew his pistol, a Glock Seventeen, a fraction of a second too late as a trio of Creeps barrelled into him, jaws snapping, claws raking. They crashed to the ground as the gun flew from his fist and landed a few feet from where I stood; he thrashed and fought the silent monsters.

Pearson dropped to one knee, and his gun cracked twice; two of the Creeps dropped, shot through the head. Fear leaping into my throat, I snatched up the fallen Glock. I had a passing familiarity with the weapon from the gun club where I practised with my L96 air-rifle, occasionally using a club loan just for a change.

A Creep came vaulting over the large tent, so I brought the gun to bear and fired; the Glock kicked in my hands, and I didn't know if I'd hit or missed. Feral eyes blazing, the Creep lashed out at me. It felt as if I had been hit in the head with a hammer. Knocked clean off my feet, I hit the ground hard, my teeth snapping together, and I rolled, frantically trying to locate the Creep through blurring vision. It reared up in front of me, arms raised above its grotesque head, clawed hands flexing for the killing blow, its mouth gaping in a silent snarl.

I saw Pearson turning in the background, his Glock raised. The barrel jerked three times, and the Creep spun away to fall bloody and lifeless in the dirt. Gratefully, I nodded thanks to Pearson just as two more Creeps burst out of the shadows between the tents. Pearson was fast; he shot one of the Creeps full in the face but missed the second. The brute was all teeth and slashing claws. Pearson fell back, the monster pinning him to the ground. Two more Creeps charged out from between the tents. Desperately, Pearson tried to bring the gun into play. Horrified, I watched the animal clamp the policeman's wrist in its jaws. With a savage jerk of its head, it severed the hand in a gout of scarlet blood. Pearson's scream was cut short as a second monster buried its teeth into his throat.

I couldn't focus; my head thundered and my hands shook violently. The gun felt like it weighed a hundred pounds as I fired blindly at the attacking monsters, the recoil nearly sent it spinning out of my grip. One of the Creeps stopped ravaging Pearson's torn and bloody body and glared at me, its mouth dripping red, claws raised as it prepared to charge.

I knew it was all over. Even if I managed to kill the first one, the other two would get me. There was no way I was going down without a fight. Raising the Glock with both hands, I took unsteady aim.

A hand fell on my shoulder, and I nearly screamed.

"Move back! Get behind me!" the soldier ordered.

I staggered back, my head reeling. I felt wet on the side of my face; the flesh there was burning hot. All I could see was Pearson, his lifeless blue eyes regarded me emptily as the soldier opened fire in three short bursts. All three Creeps fell in a swelter of dark blood; the first one almost cut in half by the fusillade.

Another Creep bounded over the roof of the tent. I opened fire. With more luck than judgment, the creature spun away as two of my bullets struck home. It hit the ground and lay still.

Dropping to one knee, the soldier emptied his automatic rifle into a group of Creeps charging across the open ground from the trees and cut them down like ripe wheat. Ejecting the spent magazine, he slammed in another and cocked the rifle, but before he had a chance to fire, two brutes leapt from the bonnet of one of the jeeps; all three fell in a slashing clawing heap.

My gun wavered at them, unable to get a clean shot. If I fired, I might hit the soldier or miss altogether. I yelled wordlessly, helplessness and frustration washing over me. The

soldier's desperate cries ended abruptly. A Creep's head snapped up, and I saw the sheen of murder in those horrific eyes. I staggered back, bumping into the cab just as the Creep launched itself at me, jaws gaping, claws reaching. I opened fire one-handed as my other hand scrabbled for the door handle. I hit the brute, knocking it sideways. It twisted in the air and landed on all fours, its awful eyes never losing sight of me. Hauling open the door, I threw myself inside and slammed the door behind me, slapping the central locking button. A split second later, the cab lurched as the Creep thudded into the side. The roof buckled as another Creep landed on top of the car. A third monster was on the bonnet, tearing off the windscreen wipers and slashing at the windshield.

Breathing heavily, I looked back to the side window. Slowly, the top of the Creep's head rose into view, then its flattened forehead, and finally, those dreadful eyes stared at me through the glass, full of hate and malice. Bloodlust swirled in the crimson depths as it silently regarded me. I shuddered.

I felt sick. My heart was racing, and my head felt as if a herd of elephants was rampaging through it. The world spun as I raised the gun, pointing it at the Creep's face mere inches away. Disorientated as I was, it would be impossible to miss at this range, but then the window would be gone.

The creature continued to stare at me, unmoving, as if it were totally unaware that it was literally looking death in the face. Maybe it was aware and didn't care. I shuddered again just as reality tipped, and everything went black.

Thirteen

November 2018
THE BLOCK

"You were lucky that day," Jules said.

"I think that's a matter of perspective," I replied, absently fingering the three-inch scar on the right side of my forehead. "It's a day I wish I could forget."

"And now you're thinking of going back out there," Jules said. "It won't be like your hunting forays, Adam. You'll be out there overnight, maybe several nights. I know the Creeps don't come out of the woodlands through the day, but we have no idea what their habits are at night when there's no sun."

"Even if they do come out at night, they still don't travel far, or they would have attacked long before now," I pointed out.

"Okay, I'll give you that," Jules conceded, "but you need to take someone with you, gain safety in numbers."

"That's not gonna happen, Jules. I won't be responsible for putting others in danger. I can do it alone," I said.

"No, you can't," the old man argued. "You need to sleep sometime, which means finding a secure location every time you stop. Still, you'll be sleeping unguarded."

"There are ways around that," I countered. "I'll travel at night, sleep during the day. I'll take one of the vans, ramp up the armour plating."

"Armour plating!" scoffed Jules. "It's corrugated iron sheets bolted to the side of the van. A concerted effort by the Creeps will tear it clean off. You know that. You've seen what they can do."

"Only if I stay in one place long enough for them to attack in force. First sign of trouble, I'll drive on."

Stumped for an opposing argument, Jules fell silent as we continued to look out over a city of shadows.

"It's not right for you to shoulder all the responsibility by yourself. We should speak with the others, put it to the vote; it's their lives as well," Jules said quietly.

"Okay, let's just say I take someone with me. Who do I take? Most of the men are married or have kids. Their families come first, and I'm definitely not taking a woman!"

"There's Derek Kaminsky?"

"Derek? Oh, come on, Jules. The man's a fruit loop. He thinks he's bloody Rambo. You've seen the frigging knife he carries about with him. It's supposed to be a covert mission, under the radar: get in, see what's there, and get out. Derek's answer to Creeps and vines is to napalm every copse, wood, and forest out of existence."

"But he would be useful if things go sideways," Jules pointed out.

"He'd probably be the cause if it went sideways in the first place; the man's about as subtle as a sledgehammer."

"Terry Moore then?"

"Jules, I appreciate what you're saying, but everyone here is a city dweller with no idea about the great outdoors. They don't know anything from city life except maybe for the odd day down at Margate. I'll be better on my own."

"Terry might have something to say about that. He thinks he owes you. After all, you saved his life," said Jules.

"Not for him to throw it away," I answered.

"Adam! Jules! You up there?"

Sally's welcome voice ended the conversation. I looked over the parapet.

"Yeah!" I called down, "What's up?"

"Stew's ready. Come and eat!"

I looked at Jules who was grinning like a Cheshire cat.

"Damn," I said, "I was looking forward to barbequed rabbit."

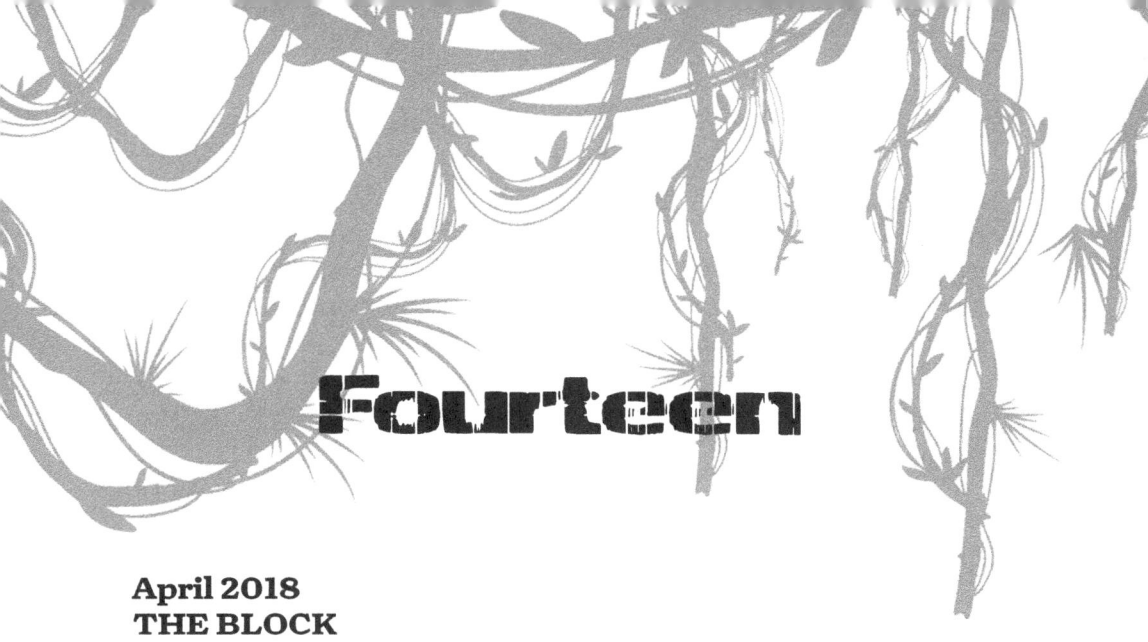

Fourteen

April 2018
THE BLOCK

Waking up wasn't a pleasant experience. The elephants were still trundling around inside my skull, my mouth was as dry as a desert, and I could hardly see. Coupled with the burning sensation on the right side of my face and nausea roiling in my guts, being out cold seemed the best option. Everything ached. Grunting, I fumbled my dysfunctional body onto the back seat of the cab off the cramped floor. Something clattered, the Glock dropping from my hand. The world swam in and out of focus as if I were viewing it through water. I was vaguely aware it was still light outside. The atmosphere inside the cab was stifling.

Digging deep, I tried to pull myself together. Wiping away the condensation misting up the windows and peering cautiously outside, there was nothing but carnage. The tents had been ripped to shredded ruin. Mutilated bodies lay in pools of congealing blood. Field tables and chairs were scattered, twisted and broken. Closing my eyes, I fought the vomit lurking at the back of my throat. Staying here wasn't an option. I had to get to the front of the cab, get away from the area, and go. *But where?* My feverish brain couldn't deal with such a complex question right now.

There was no sign of any Creeps nearby. *Are they cunning enough to lie in wait? Do they have that sort of mentality?* Another question too complex to consider. Reaching down for the Glock, I popped the magazine, fully expecting it to be empty. I was surprised, or maybe relieved, to discover it still had four of its seventeen round load. My rifle was in the passenger well of the cab, but I seriously doubted its stopping power. Besides, it would be too slow.

Forcing my protesting body into a sitting position, I looked around the cab's perimeter; everything was still. My right hand stole towards the door handle, the gun ready in my left. I tried to lick my lips, but my tongue was sticky and clung to the roof of my mouth.

"Shit, shit, shit," I croaked. My heart felt as if it was fit to burst out of my chest. With a deep breath, I threw open the door, hurling myself onto the ground. Landing on my back, tracking the gun anywhere a Creep might be lurking: the roof of the cab, by the jeeps, amongst the debris of the tents.

Nothing.

Breathing heavily and feeling vulnerable outside the safety of the cab, I got to my feet. Moving amongst the detritus strewn around the command post, it was obvious there was nothing to be done for Pearson or the dead soldiers. Sorrow washed over me as I looked over the torn and mutilated bodies. Taking Pearson's gun belt and holster, I moved from body to body, salvaging their spare ammunition, covering their remains with bits of canvas from the tents. The automatic weapons were useless to me; there were no spare magazines. Some of the rifles had been smashed and rendered inoperable, presumably by the Creeps who in a mindless rage recognised them as the engines of their destruction. Besides, I had no experience with the weapons, so I left them where they lay.

Loading a full magazine into the Glock, I holstered it. The belt was a comforting weight about my waist. The rest of the spare magazines went into the passenger well of the cab. As I got in behind the wheel, my body was soaked in sweat, and I could smell my own sour stench. Every movement became a painful exertion as I rested my throbbing head on the steering wheel. The park was ominously quiet, no gunfire from the woods and no blaze of flamethrowers from across the lake.

In my delirium, I considered leaning on the cab's horn to alert anyone close enough to my situation, but instinct warned me that was all kinds of wrong; the only attention it would attract would be of the tooth and claw variety. I would report the incident at the security barrier and let the soldiers deal with it.

Slowing, I approached the Whitehouse Roundabout. The barriers were gone. One was smashed, scattered across the tarmac; the other lay on the kerb across the road. The army sergeant who so kindly allowed me through was propped up against the low wall supporting the wrought iron fence surrounding the park. I didn't need to get any closer to see that the man was dead. There was no sign of the other soldiers.

A violent shudder tore through me, nausea welled up again, and bitter bile flooded my mouth. Heedless of the danger, I opened the door and threw up into the street. The bile burned my throat, exacerbated the pain in my chest. Spitting out the last of the vile liquid, I wiped my mouth, closed the door, and drove on.

I was feeling bad, really bad. The road ahead blurred as I continually swiped at my watering eyes. With gritted teeth, I tried to focus, concentrate on driving, but I was shivering so much it was a miracle I didn't crash. Whether it was sheer luck or some blind instinct, I found myself back at Buckingham Avenue. I staggered out of the cab. The street was buckling under my feet, the houses rippled, and the bright blue sky was spinning. Striking the front door with my shoulder, I grunted and dropped to my knees, vaguely aware that I had my keys in my hand and was fumbling for the lock. Getting the door open was a blur as I dragged myself over the threshold. Before me loomed a wavering mountain of stairs seemingly going up and up forever. On hands and knees, I crawled forward, my body screaming at me with every movement. Inside my head, the elephants rampaged wildly.

"Fuck," I mumbled. "Fuck…"

I was on the floor staring at dust bunnies under the bed. Light slanted through the bedroom window. *Is it late evening or early morning?* I had no idea. I knew I didn't want to move. Lying there on the carpet, there was no pain, no aching joints, and no thundering elephants. I was afraid that the euphoric feeling would leave me if I tried to get up. The point became moot as pins and needles attacked my right arm which was pinned beneath my body. Rolling over onto my back, I groaned, my worst fears realised.

"Fuck." I was using that word a lot lately; it was becoming my mantra.

The cursing was warranted as a chorus of pain sang through my entire body, centering on my face and stomach. My jeans, cold and wet, clung to me uncomfortably.

"Wonderful," I mumbled, looking down at the darker material around my crotch and thighs. I'd pissed myself.

Unhitching the gun belt around my waist felt ten tons lighter, and I sat up, groaning loudly. Too fast, the room spun. Remaining still in a sitting position, eyes closed, chin on my chest, I waited until the bedroom righted itself. Getting to my feet was a struggle, but getting my dirty, pissed-soaked clothes off was a bigger struggle. Somehow, I managed it.

Thirst ravaged my throat, but the kitchen seemed too far away, so I staggered to the bathroom. I was shivering violently, even though my body felt as if it were burning up with fever; my skin felt greasy with sweat. I almost fell into the bathtub as my fingers groped the faucet. My scream echoed around the tiled room as icy cold water cascaded over my shocked body. It took my breath away, killing the scream in my constricted vocal cords. Gripping the side of the tub, I forced myself to kneel there, head down, gasping for breath until, bizarrely, I began to feel warm.

Grabbing one of the towels from the rail, I spread it as much as I could on the floor. I got the second towel and tumbled out of the tub to lay breathless on the floor.

"Oh fuck." The word was like an old friend.

The shower had invigorated me temporarily even though fever still raged inside me. My face still ached as I sat on the edge of the bed trying to regain some of the strength used in getting dressed. Looking in the mirror, I didn't recognise the battered and haggard face staring back at me with bleary dark eyes and sunken hollow cheeks sporting what looked like three days of beard growth.

Jesus, how long was I out?

There was a three-inch laceration on the right-hand side of my forehead, an ugly wound which looked infected, inflamed, red and black bruising, a whitish ichor oozing from the open cut. This I deemed as the source of the fever, inflicted by the damned Creep's claws. Getting some alcohol and gauze from the medicine cabinet, I cleaned it as best I could, finally covering it with a sterile pad and securing it with Band-Aid. It seemed to take forever as focusing was still a problem.

Exhausted, I lay back on the bed, rolled myself up in the duvet, and slept.

I was dying. I knew it as sure as eggs. At first, I didn't understand, but then I knew. The Creeps. They were like the vines: venomous, their bite, their claws. The toxin wasn't as virulent as the vines; it worked slower but with the same inevitable outcome.

How I was thinking with such clarity I didn't know, and it didn't matter. What mattered was getting help fast. My body was unresponsive, wracked with aches and pain so deep it reached down into my very soul. My joints felt as if they were packed with ground glass; my muscles were like jelly. Languishing here wasn't going to help me. The longer I waited, the weaker I got. I had to move. The only place that could help me was already a designated a safe area, and I had to get somehow or someway to Queen Elizabeth Hospital.

I went down the stairs on my arse after dragging my tortured body across the bedroom floor on my belly. My balance was shot. I was running on autopilot, making it up as I went along. I regretted downing half a bottle of water earlier; my stomach was heaving, but I had been so dry, so hot. Already, sweat soaked my clothes.

The cab was parked askew across the pavement practically outside my door. Using the door jamb, I got to my feet. Weirdly, I centred on the paving stones on the pavement; they were literally rising, becoming uneven as green showed in the cracks, purple-black tendrils creeping out beneath the concrete. *Is my imagination playing tricks or is it really happening?* Like everything else outside of the pain,

I couldn't deal with it now, mentally or otherwise. Tearing my eyes away, I staggered into the street and clambered into the cab.

"Gotta rest, gotta rest," I mumbled, leaning on the steering wheel.

A disconcerting thought crept unbidden into my pounding head: a memory, David Baxter's voice, low, full of grief.

"There was nothing they could do. They couldn't identify the venom that was systematically shutting down all her bodily functions..."

With an angry twist of the wrist, I started the cab, reversed off the kerb, put it into drive, and headed for the hospital. I'd run out of choices and time was following suit. What was left gave me little hope.

I was fucked.

Fifteen

April 2018

I lay quiet in the restful darkness, immobile, relaxed, and
serene. My body was warm, which was a blessing because I
had no more strength left to fight the chills that had plagued
me for so long. I wanted to stay just as I was right at that
moment, at peace. It seemed like forever since I had felt
such peace, a lifetime ago. Maybe it was because I had surrendered, let go. It was liberating. It was a relief.

I had no memory of how I had reached this final point,
nor was there any sense of where I was. I didn't care.

Just to finally be at peace.

Sixteen

April 2018

I wasn't dead. I've got to say I was surprised. I lay in a bed in a room, a normal room, someone's bedroom, and I was alive. Recent experience prevented me from wanting to move. Except for feeling as weak as a kitten, I was pain free. The bedroom was dimly lit, and I couldn't make out details. I was lying in the centre of a very comfortable double bed with clean sheets up to my chest covering my nakedness; my arms rested on top of the sheet. I felt a little like a corpse. I could see a water jug and glass on the bedside cabinet; suddenly, I was very thirsty. I definitely wasn't dead.

A flickering, ruddy light played on the closed curtains. I'd seen enough campfires in my time to know what it was, but not why. It was puzzling, but the mystery could wait. I needed a drink.

Grunting, I tried to sit up and discovered it was not a good idea as I flopped back onto the pillows, completely sapped of strength. The water was tantalisingly close, taunting me, catching the light of the fire from outside dancing in its clear depths. Teeth clenched, muscles cracking, the tendons popping out on my neck, I tried again.

"Hey, hey, lie down. You need to keep still."

The cheerful, mildly chastising voice surprised me as I relaxed back onto the bed. A woman appeared by the bed and poured some water for me, propping my head as I gratefully drank. She regarded me with caring blue eyes, a small smile on her full mouth set in an attractive face framed by shoulder-length, flaming red hair.

"Slowly, Adam. Not too much." She took the glass away, returning it to the bedside cabinet.

Taking my wrist, she studied her watch.

"Thank you," I croaked.

"You're welcome," she said, releasing my wrist. "How are you feeling?"

"Weak." I tried to smile but failed.

"Not surprising. We'll soon have you right as rain. Oh, I'm Sally by the way. I'll be back in a little while with some soup for you. Meanwhile, rest."

And then she was gone.

The chicken soup was amazing. Okay, I was starving, but that didn't depreciate how good it tasted. Sally sat on the bed spoon feeding me, and I savoured every drop.

"You'll be on solids soon enough," she said, wiping my mouth. "Get some meat on your bones."

"Where am I?" I asked. "How did I get here?"

"Well, here is the Block, a quaint name for the New Leaf Sheltered Project, which is pretty ironic when you consider the circumstances. You've been under my care for the last eight days."

"Eight days?" I queried, dumbfounded.

"Yep, not counting however long you were wandering around out there," Sally said. "It was lucky you were found when you were, though Jules might not think so." Sally smiled at some private joke.

"Jules?"

"Jules Robideaux. He was the one who found you, or rather you found him. You nearly ran him over."

"Oh my God! I didn't..."

Sally brushed my concern aside. "No, the old fool's light on his feet. Besides, you were hardly moving."

"Where was this?" I asked, mortified.

"Right outside the Block," Sally said.

"Oh man, tell him I'm sorry. I..."

"No worries, Adam. Once he saw the state of you, any dent in his dignity ceased to matter."

I frowned. "How do you know my name?"

"Ah," Sally said, pulling back the curtains and allowing daylight in, "there's a riddle for you." She gathered up the tray. "It seems your reputation precedes you."

"What?"

Chuckling, she left the room.

A gentle knocking at the door woke me from a doze. A dark head poked into the room.

"Come in. I'm awake," I said.

"I wasn't sure. I didn't want to disturb you," said the aging black man.

He was getting on, I figured early sixties, close cropped hair with more than just a little grey, his eyes dark and intelligent.

"I can come back later," he said hesitantly.

"No, it's fine. I'd be glad of the company," I encouraged.

Picking up a chair, he placed it by the bed. "You're looking a lot better," he said as he sat down.

"Chicken soup." I smiled.

He laughed, a deep rich sound. "That'd be Sally, one of the Lord's wonders."

"So it seems," I agreed.

"I'm Jules," he said, extending his hand.

I took his hand briefly. "My saviour," I said, "that I nearly ran down. I'm really sorry."

He flapped his bony hand in the air. "No problem. The cab was hardly moving. Thirty years ago, I would have stopped you barehanded."

I believed him. As old as he was, you could still see the robust, athletic man he must have been in his youth.

"I guess I didn't make it to Queen Elizabeth's then?" I said. "Where did I end up?"

"You're just outside of Woolwich, back of Herbert Road. It's a sheltered community, though I'm the only resident left."

"Sally said, but how the hell did I get here? I was heading for the hospital."

"It's pretty crazy out there, lots of confusion, blocked roads. Most of the people evacuated to either Queen

Elizabeth's or Greenwich Hospitals. The area's all but deserted," Jules said.

"I thought I was dead for sure," I said.

"Because of your head wound?" Jules asked. "No, it just made you really sick. Sally's a district nurse. She worked at the hospital for a while.

"She tended a few wounds like yours, some scratches, mainly bites. They're not fatal, though you seemed to have a particularly nasty allergic reaction to it."

"Gotta say it felt like dying," I said glumly.

Jules chuckled. "Sally wouldn't have let anything bad happen to you, not on her watch. Fierce lady!"

"I can believe it. She seems like a force of nature," I began.

"Who does?" Sally was standing at the door.

"Woman, you know better than to eavesdrop!" Jules said, turning in his chair. "You'll never hear good of yourself!"

"You're mistaking me for someone who cares, Old Man." Sally laughed. "Anyway, I wasn't eavesdropping; I've got someone here who's been waiting to see Adam."

"Who?" I said.

Sally stepped aside.

"Charlie!" I exclaimed.

Charlie was across the room in an instant, grasping my hand.

"Hello, mate," he said happily. "You definitely know how to put a scare into a bloke. Jeez Adam, look at you!"

"What are you doing here? How'd you find me?" I asked, still not believing my eyes.

"Long story," Charlie said. "Short version is that we evacuated to Queen Elizabeth's and that was our first mistake. It was organised chaos there—so many people, not enough resources. We stuck it out for three days with hardly any food in cramped quarters, all four of us in a little box room with hardly enough room to swing a cat. Anyway, when you didn't show, we started to get worried, so we decided to come looking for you."

"We?" I asked.

"Yeah, Julie and the kids are with me."

"Christ, Charlie, that's a big risk. You should have stayed where it was safe," I protested.

"You didn't see it there, Adam. I'm not joking when I say there wasn't anywhere near enough personnel organising the place. They didn't have a clue what was going on. Then the crazy rumours started flying about. There was talk of further evacuation, commandeering cruise ships and oil tankers, getting out to sea. Another one said we were moving to Central London as soon as the soldier boys had torched everything green. Julie and I talked about it, and it seemed more sense to head back to Buckingham Avenue to sort ourselves out."

"Not a good idea, Charlie. Trust me, I've seen it. How did you find me here?" I asked.

"Your cab," he said. "We couldn't get through Shooters Hill Road, so we came the long way around through Woolwich, being pushed further and further south, blocked roads, stalled traffic, abandoned vehicles, and of course, avoiding green areas. Making for Red Lion Hill, David spotted your cab parked on the side of the road. We stopped for a looksee, and a young lady saw us and told us you were here."

"That was Teresa," Sally chipped in.

"Yeah, Teresa, and well, here we are," Charlie finished.

"And welcome," Jules added.

"So, what the hell happened to you?" Charlie asked. "Gotta say, mate, you looked awful when I first saw you, pale as ice cream. That was what, four days ago? You're looking a lot better now."

"Thanks to Sally," I said. "It was bad, Charlie, really bad."

"Did you find Linda?" he asked.

"No, I found her house, but there was no one there," I hesitated, reluctant to go on. "Charlie, I met Colin Pearson at the park. We were attacked."

I told him about the events at the park as everyone listened in grim silence.

"All of them dead?" Charlie said quietly. "Space monkeys won out over automatic weapons and flamethrowers? That's impossible."

"Colin called them 'Creeps,'" I said. "They would have gotten me too if not for that soldier. I don't even know his name. They don't fight one on one, but in coordinated attacks, one, two, three, four at a time. I swear they used the trees as a distraction, making us think they were there right before they attacked."

"You think they're intelligent?" asked Jules.

"Maybe not intelligent," I answered. "More instinctive, like wolves or lions when they hunt, working as a team."

"There you go, spouting that nature stuff again," Charlie said, half joking.

"It's what I saw," I told him.

"Okay, I think that's enough," Sally said. "Adam still needs to rest. Come on, out. All of you!"

Jules put the chair back. "We'll talk some more later," he said as he left.

"It's good to see you," Charlie said, "and don't worry about your cab. I brought it into the square and covered it with a tarpaulin. You had some interesting items in the passenger well; you might want to tell me about them when you're up to it." He winked as he followed Jules out the door.

"Rest," Sally ordered, and then I was alone again.

And I did rest. I thought I was all rested up, and I felt as if a great weight had been lifted off my shoulders; I could breathe again. I was determined about one thing: no more bedpans. Sally argued, but I won. Looking back, I think she let me win.

The skeleton looking back at me from the bathroom mirror was a stranger. I must have lost twenty pounds; my ribs were showing, my face a bearded skull, the eyes sunken wells, my hair almost down to my shoulders.

"Jesus…" I said softly.

"Don't worry," Sally said from the bathroom door. "After a couple of days of good food and plenty of fluids, you'll be back to your old self."

The following day I was on my feet. I felt a little woozy, but I wasn't going to tell Sally that. She'd be clucking around me like an old mother hen trying to get me back into bed. I discovered I was in Sally's two-bedroom flat. Oddly, the décor and paintings on the walls, scenes of windmills and seascapes, didn't match her bubbly personality. She told me all the people living in the Block had commandeered abandoned flats as their own. All except Jules, who was the only legitimate resident.

"I was his district nurse, have been for the last seven years," Sally explained. "When the proverbial hit the fan, I came to check on him. The stubborn, old fool refused to leave his home when they evacuated all the other residents. Considering recent events, maybe Jules knew more than he was saying. Anyway, I ended up staying too."

"Have you no family?" I asked.

"No, I had a husband until ten years ago, useless lump. I think we were both glad to see the back of each other. We never had children." She offered me a pair of jeans. "These should fit."

I looked at her.

"Oh, come on! I'm a nurse!" She laughed. "Besides, who do you think put you to bed in the first place, not to mention bed baths."

I got dressed, blushing only slightly.

Quite a reception was waiting for me when we went out into the square. Thirty or so people had congregated outside the flat. Julie came over and hugged me.

"I'm so glad you're okay." She smiled. "You had us all worried."

"Uncle Adam!" David and Juney rushed forward, each hugging a leg.

"Uncle?" I asked, looking at Charlie.

"Don't look at me; they're the ones who adopted you!" He laughed.

I knelt and hugged them both.

"You've met Jules," said Sally. "This is Teresa Wright."

A young woman with light brown hair and sad blue eyes nodded timidly at me.

"This is Tom Taylor and his boys, Andrew, Paul and Stephen."

The introductions went on, and I knew I wouldn't remember all their names but would in time.

One thing all these people had in common was that they were broken. They had lost family, friends, husbands, wives, and children. There was a discernible sadness surrounding them all which came together in this place. Hope was the only thing left to them, so they clung to one another, all with the same desperate look in their eyes. Hope that their loved ones may return looking for them, and afraid to leave in case that last hope withered. I thought of Linda. *Where could she be?* I surprised myself at still thinking of her and pondered the sudden ache in my heart.

"So, you're the one causing all the ruckus!" came a voice from behind me.

I turned. "Tina!"

She stood there beaming at me, the twins, Mark and Matthew, by her side.

"You didn't think you were going to get rid of me that easily, did you?" she said, hugging me. "Welcome back to the land of the living!"

Seventeen

May 2018

The next three weeks were busy. Under Sally's watchful care, I regained both my weight and my strength until I was able to move into my own flat, becoming the only person on the first floor of the Block. Charlie and some of the others had cleared it out and prepared it for me. It felt odd living in someone else's home. I wondered who had lived there and where they were now. Would they ever return? Somehow, I didn't think so.

It was a relief to have a hot shower and to finally shave off my damned beard, though I kept the long hair. Sally offered to cut it for me, but I kind of liked the hippie look. All the occupied flats had electricity courtesy of Tom Taylor and his son, Andrew. Being electricians, it was easy for them to wire in petrol-fuelled generators salvaged from the surrounding engineering warehouses and shops to the Block's electric circuits, giving lights, electric stoves, and hot water.

Reports were coming in that a lot of the roads and streets were in a bad way and getting worse by the day. Vines had wheedled their way beneath the tarmac and concrete, getting closer and closer to the Block, buckling the roadways, tearing up the tarmac. It was making the supply runs more and more difficult and dangerous. Supplies were brought in from everywhere. Going mobile with one of the generators in a Transit panel van, Tom and his son were able to power up the pumps at petrol stations. They stored several hundred gallons of petrol in a brick building at the rear of the Block which was originally used for large, now defunct, dustbins.

Canned and dry goods were stored in three of the flats on the first floor. Several of the big supermarkets were dotted around the area, notably a large Sainsbury's which had a large, fully stocked warehouse. The downside was there was no fresh meat. We found freezers, but the meat was rotten and stank to high heaven.

I found it puzzling that The Block still had a water supply. All the other amenities had been shut down weeks ago. *Why not water?* With the stores, generators, and water supplies, the Block was pretty much self-sufficient. Still, it wasn't all a bed of roses, pardon the pun.

Further reports, more and more disturbing, were coming back from our patrols. The vines were prolific; the parks were overrun. We were being surrounded.

"We need to do something," Tom Taylor said. "Sooner or later, someone's going to get killed by those damned things."

"Then we burn them," Jules said. "We've more than enough petrol. We'll take four or five vehicles loaded with petrol bombs and fry their arses."

So that's what we did.

Armed with wooden crates full of petrol bombs, four cars and Tom's van went out into the streets and burned every vine we could. We had to be careful; the fires had to be controlled since the last thing we wanted was to set fire to the houses.

I was getting restless and needed to get out. I wanted to go and see the surrounding area for myself. Taking my rifle from the closet, I checked that it was loaded. Charlie had put the holstered Glock and ammunition he found in the cab into a wooden box and locked it with a small padlock on a high shelf in the closet. After checking the pistol, I belted it around my waist. Flashes of that day in the park flickered onto the screen in my mind, and I hastily pushed them away. Taking a canteen of water and a packed lunch, I headed for the cab.

"Where you off to, Sunshine?" Charlie asked as I crossed the courtyard.

"Just a little me time, Charlie. Getting a little bit of cabin fever," I answered.

"You're not going into the parks, are you?" he asked, eyeing the guns.

"No, mate." I gave a brief smile. "I'm gonna keep my distance, but something's been bothering me. Need to check it out."

"Oh? What?" he asked, falling in beside me.

"We've got people going out on a regular basis, all reporting vine incursions, right?"

He nodded.

"In all these weeks, no one's reported seeing any Creeps. It's got me wondering," I said.

"Maybe they've all died like in that Tom Cruise film, *War of the Worlds*," Charlie suggested.

"Nice thought," I agreed, "but I don't think so. I'm going to have a look anyway."

It was a lovely May morning, clear sky and warmer than normal for this time of year, but I wasn't about to complain. Sweat was already gathering under my arms. The denim jacket I was wearing was unnecessary, but I didn't want the children to see the Glock. It was good to see the kids playing and enjoying themselves in the sunshine. Their laughter was music on the air. As they played, the adults worked. Mothers hung out washing on lines strung between wooden poles; others talked and laughed as they swept the walkways or cleaned windows. Everyone kept a watchful eye on the children. In one corner, Trish Morgan had improvised a temporary classroom. It was too nice to be inside, so they used boxes for seats and camping tables for desks. An art lesson was in progress for the younger children: finger painting, lots of bright colour, tons of mess. It made me smile.

Roger Boulter, our resident mechanic, was working on one of the three vans we had acquired; Stephen Taylor assisted him. Jeff Shepherd and Alan Holden were unloading another van, fresh in from a provision foray. It could have been just an ordinary day in an ordinary suburb of London, friends and neighbours enjoying quality time together. I saw with my heart, but my mind reminded me that it was an illusion.

"Where are you intending to go?" Charlie asked.

"Honestly?" I said, stowing the gear in the cab. "I'm heading back towards Denford Park, and you can take that worried look off your face. I'm not intending to get out of the cab; I just want to look."

"Maybe I should come with you."

"No, Charlie. You're all right. I'll be back before you know it."

It was weird driving in the empty streets. Not because of the absence of people but because of the unnatural silence. It felt more like early morning than almost noon. The temperature was rising, making me thankful for the cab's AC. My jean jacket was on the back seat, and my bare arms were slick with sweat, despite the air conditioning.

Once outside the half mile perimeter we had set, the scorched earth ceased and the vines became apparent, pushing up beneath the pavements, warping the road's tarmac. Slithering, snake-like, they fought for existence, cracking the concrete like eggshells. Eventually, a solution to the vines would have to be found before their hold on the land became unassailable. Thoughts of fire and Agent Orange stole into my mind, and I wondered if the cure would be worse than the disease.

Whitehouse Roundabout was a no-go. Vines had already reclaimed the wrought iron fencing surrounding Denford Park and encroached across the road to join with the vines fronting the row of semi-detached houses. I turned around, noting with distaste that the body of the soldier was no longer propped against the wall of the park. Circling around, I got to Park Vista Road on the north side. The park was now on my right as I drove slowly down the road. A dense copse of oaks lined the park fence which was totally enveloped with vines like sickly emerald and purple drapes spilling out onto the wide pavements, spreading, ever spreading.

Deep shadows pooled beneath the trees accentuated by the bright sunlight. Peering closer, I was sure there was something lurking in the lower branches. Pulling over, I got the telescopic sight off my rifle and exited the cab. I had to lay my denim jacket over the bonnet of the cab since the metal was searing hot, too much for my bare arms. Resting my elbows, I sighted the lens and brought the trees into focus.

What the fuck?

It was unbelievable.

Adjusting the focus, I looked again. There were dozens, maybe hundreds, squatting in the branches of the vine-infested wrought iron fencing, seemingly impervious to the lethal thorns, perfectly, uncannily still, regarding me with murderous black and red eyes. Creeps. My heart was pounding in my chest as I panned along the line of trees. Every branch and bough was occupied by glaring monsters, still as statues. Some clung to the tree trunks, every crimson eye looking straight at me with an unflinching gaze.

Sweet Jesus...

I don't know what suddenly possessed me. Taking the rifle from the back seat, I refitted the telescopic sight, cocked the rifle, and took aim. The crosshairs flitted from one brute to another, finally resting on one that seemed a little bigger than the rest of its gruesome companions. It sat unheeding on the branch just under two hundred feet away. It was close to the rifle's effective range, and I truly doubted it would be a killing shot, but I was angry. I don't know why. Maybe I did, but I didn't care why. I felt offended.

Calming down, I resighted on the Creep, pushing all thoughts out of my head. I took a deep breath and slowly squeezed the trigger. The Creep tumbled off the branch, but my shout of jubilation died in my throat as its body seemed to stop in mid-air. Confused, I looked through the scope, gasping in shock. The brute hung from a branch by one muscular hand, expressionless, unruffled, its eyes boring into mine through the telescopic sight. With a twist of its body, the Creep somersaulted back onto the branch and settled into its previous position.

This isn't possible. Out of the dozens of possible targets, how could the Creep have known I was aiming at him? And then to evade the shot so easily?

Cold gripped my body My mind was blank as I tried to come to terms with the repercussions of what just happened, unable to believe. Slowly, I pulled my jacket off the bonnet, returning it and my rifle to the rear seat and got into the front. My fingers played against the Glock, and I had the sudden urge to blast away at the monsters, send them all back to the hell they had come from, see if they could evade concentrated fire. But what if they did? Oh my god. It didn't bear thinking about. Then I remembered what Charlie had said about the Creeps winning out over flamethrowers and automatic weapons.

Heading back, still in shock, I decided to make a visit to Buckingham Avenue. I needed time to clear my head and make sense of it all; driving had always helped with that. I remembered my binoculars were in the bedside cabinet where I had put them after a session of watching the night sky before the black Dust descended upon Wellingham.

The street was a mess, the roadway like all the others I had traversed, buckled and cracked, paving stones drunk and askew, young vines pushing their way inexorably into the light. Not wanting to take any chances, I mounted the kerb and parked a car door's width from the flat. I stepped over the gap and hurried upstairs.

The place smelled musty, earthy almost; it didn't feel like home anymore. Retrieving the binoculars, I looked around for the last time. I had liked living here, but in truth, it never felt like home. Nowhere did to me. It was as if I was fated to be ever on the move, living from one place to the next. That suited me fine. Though I preferred to do it of my own volition, not because I was forced.

Sighing, I went downstairs.

Shit!

The vines clung to both sides of the door jamb. Others slithered out from beneath the cab, wavering back and forth as if tasting the air. There was no way pass them. If I tried, the thorns would stick me for sure. The cab's open door was a tantalising few feet away; with maybe one quick dash, I'd be past the vines before they could react. Then I remembered the speed the vine had struck at the roundabout.

I needed inspiration to get through the vines. I looked around the flat. A can of tent weatherproofing spray lay beside the open door of the landing cupboard. Shaking the can, I went to my kitchen junk drawer, a drawer that I was sure every household had, and fished out a disposable lighter. As I approached the vines, they became more agitated. One lashed out at me, fast as whipcord, but it was nowhere near long enough.

"Fuck you too!" I grated, depressing the can's button and flicking on the lighter.

The effect was instantaneous; the vines writhed and burned, twisting away from the flames. I dived for the driver's seat, slamming the cab door behind me, stuck it into drive, and left Buckingham Avenue behind me for good.

The high street was in shambles. Rubbish was piled everywhere, and several shopping carts displaying Tesco's red and blue brand name lay sprawled on the pavements; one lay in the shattered ruins of a clothes shop window. I saw signs of looting for the first time. The electronics shop next to Carpetright's had no windows; DVD players and laptops lay broken amidst the shattered glass. The jewellers had been looted, too. Oddly, the independent grocery store three shops down selling exotic foodstuffs from Jamaica and the West Indies was untouched. Making a mental note of Morrison's Supermarket and the Tesco Hypermarket, I carried on to Westwood Lane. I'd seen enough and wanted to go home.

There were a few cars standing forlorn in the community car park at the corner of Westwood Lane and the High Street. Vines were swarming over the dividing wall at the rear, separating the car park from the allotment holdings. A line of sycamore trees threw shadows over the far corner.

The banging was intermittent, wood on metal, getting louder as I turned into Westwood. Powering down the window, the banging became clearer and sounded angry. It emanated from the alley leading up to the allotments where I could see something moving in the shadows, the glare of the sun making it difficult to see details. Using the dividing wall as cover and keeping low, I crouched in the mouth of the alley. Sixty feet into the alley, outside the vine infested gates of the allotments, three Creeps were beating on a large metal wheelie bin with lengths of heavy wood; one had a thick branch. The Glock was in my hand without conscious thought. I had no idea what they were doing, and I didn't want to know as I slowly backed off. This was no place to be.

The screams were loud, shrill, filled with terror. Someone was trapped in the bin! *How were they managing to keep the lid closed against the Creeps?* It was only a matter of time before the brutes prevailed and reached their prey. I edged closer, training the Glock on the unsuspecting Creeps as they beat their awful cacophony on the bin. Getting as close as I dared, I dropped to one knee.

I opened fire, blasting away before the terror overcame me. Two of the Creeps dropped like stones. The third managed a half turn before my bullets tore the life out of it, its bloodied body falling across its lifeless companions.

Fighting the hyperventilation, I hurried forward keeping the gun on the fallen monsters, taking no chances. The lid of the rubbish bin was still locked shut.

"Out! Now!" I shouted, banging on the bin with my fist.

A terrified whimpering was the only response.

"For fuck's sake! Open the fucking lid!" I was practically screaming. "We need to get out of here fast!"

"No, no! The monsters..." the voice pleaded.

"They're dead, and so will we be if you don't fucking get out of there! Move, or I swear I'll leave you. Open the lid."

There was a scraping sound as I threw open the lid, and a young boy shied away in terror.

"Dammit!"

I hauled him out and let him fall in the dirt next to the dead Creeps. He screamed and scooted back on his hands. Grabbing him by his filthy tee-shirt, I dragged him along the alley and threw him into the back of the cab. He scrabbled into the corner, folding up into a fetal position and covering his face. There was no time for pity. I started the cab, gunned the engine, and headed for home.

Eighteen

May 2018

"Is he okay?" I asked, getting up from the sofa.

"Yes," said Sally, wiping her hands on a towel as she came into the sitting room. "Frightened, dehydrated, but he'll be all right given time."

"Did you get a name?" asked Jules from the armchair.

"No, he hasn't said a word." Sally gratefully accepted a cup of tea from Tina. "There's no ID on him either."

"You certainly know how to have a good time, don't you, mate?" Charlie said to me.

"I could do without 'em, Charlie. Trust me," I answered. "It's got me thinking though."

"About what?" Jules asked.

"This place," I said. "Security is non-existent. We need to rethink our defences."

"Defences? Against what? The Creeps?" Tina asked.

"For a start, yes," I said. "When they attacked in the park, they came at us bare-handed; today they were using clubs. When I saw them in the trees, they were acting unnatural, just sitting there staring at me. It was unlike any animal behaviour I've ever seen or heard of."

"And you would know," chipped in Charlie.

I gave him a look, and he just grinned.

"I'm serious," I said. "Despite the burnings, the vines are flourishing, and with the vines come the Creeps. If ever they reach the Block in its present state, we'll never be able to hold them back."

"Why not?" asked Sally. "There's only two ways in or out."

"Look behind you," I said. "That window leads directly outside. All around the perimeter, there are windows looking out over the street, making easy access in any assault."

"Are you suggesting we board up all the windows?" asked Jules. "It'll be like living in a cave. All our natural light comes from those windows. There's precious little allowed in from the courtyard."

"Maybe not boarded up but secured. Maybe we could bolt heavy mesh through the walls. There's also several drainpipes that lead to the roof, so we'll need to secure those, string them with barbed wire to make them inaccessible," I said.

"We'd be turning our home into a fortress," said Tina.

"Better to have it and never need it than need it and not have it," I said.

"What about the archway? We can't seal that off, and there's no one skilled enough to build a suitable gate," Jules said.

"There's a simpler solution to that," I replied. "We'll get a bus, armour one side, then we'll have a mobile gate."

The boy just slept, troubled by dreams that had him screaming himself awake, wild-eyed and sweating, thrashing about, and throwing off the bed clothes. Sally calmed him, but he refused to talk, eating only meagre meals and sipping the minimum of water before going back to sleep.

On the second evening since finding the boy, we were outside Sally's flat having a beer and reviewing the ongoing security work. Tom Taylor remembered seeing some sheets of heavy-duty mesh at one of the engineering works he and his boys had raided. It turned out there was more than enough for our needs. They also found several boxes of carriage bolts long enough to go through the walls enabling secure fixings for the mesh. I saw the work; it was impressive, strong, and it gave peace of mind.

The drainpipes were strung with razor wire, and the roof's parapets were crowned just below the top edges, denying access to the roof.

Teresa Wright came over and joined the group. Saying nothing, she sat quietly listening at the periphery. Eventually, the talk returned to the newcomer.

"He doesn't look a day over nineteen, maybe twenty," said Sally. "As thin as a rake."

"Do you think he's local?" asked Jules.

"There's no way of knowing," Sally said. "He's so traumatised."

"Being trapped in a rubbish bin by three rampaging monsters is enough to traumatise anyone," I said. "Judging by the state of him, he hasn't had it easy. It's possible he's had to fend for himself since all this started."

"It'll take patience," Sally said, "but I'm sure we'll be able to get through to him. We'll just have to let him go at his own pace."

"Could I talk to him?" Teresa said.

Sally looked surprised. "Do you think you know him?" she asked.

"No," said Teresa, "I just thought it might help if someone with the same sort of experience talked to him."

Glances were exchanged. Teresa was one of the few living at the Block whose history was unknown.

"Well, I'm sure it won't hurt," Sally said, looking at her watch. "It's about time for his evening meal. Would you like to bring it to him?"

Teresa nodded, following Sally into the flat.

"So," said Charlie, "you think there's another group out there somewhere?"

"I don't know if they're still around, but there were definite signs of looting in Wellingham."

"Could they be trouble?" asked Tom.

"We can only hope not," I said. "Should we come across them, we'll just have to keep our guard up till we're sure one way or the other."

"What about our future?" Tina asked. "We're okay in the short term, but what about a year from now? Two years? What are we going to do?"

"You're talking as if there is no solution to the vines," said Jules.

"Do you think there is?" Tina asked.

"We can only survive at the moment," Jules said. "Take one day at a time. Sooner or later, someone in authority is going to show up and give us back our lives."

"You really believe that?" I asked.

"I have to," Jules said passionately. "I have to believe in something, or what's the point in going on?"

"And what if no one turns up? What if we're on our own?" Charlie asked.

"Then I'd have to do some hard thinking," said Jules.

"Maybe we should draw up some contingency plans to relocate should that eventuality ever arise," I suggested.

"Where would we go?" asked Tom.

"We'd have to work that out; somewhere there isn't a lot of green. As Tina pointed out, we're well supplied right now, but that's finite. If we don't get relief, or the vine and Creep problem isn't resolved, we're going to have to think about becoming self-sufficient, both industrially and agriculturally."

"You mean become farmers?" Charlie said. "Jesus, mate, what do we know about farming?"

"Well, I know a little," I said.

"Of course, you do!" Charlie laughed. "Why am I not surprised at that?"

"I'm no expert, Charlie. We'll have to research, but it's an option."

"Isn't that a contradiction?" asked Tina. "Keeping away from the green areas but becoming farmers?"

"A good trick if you can do it." Charlie grinned, looking at me with a twinkle in his eye.

"It's something for us all to think about," I said.

"Have you somewhere in mind?" asked Jules.

"Not exactly. I keep thinking concrete jungle, and Thamesmead comes to mind," I said.

There were groans and frowns all round.

"See?" I said. "We all know Thamesmead is a shithole, hardly any parks or greenery, a concrete jungle. The River Thames runs along the eastern border which could be a plus for us."

"How the hell do we farm on concrete?" asked Tom.

"There are various methods, but I would think raised beds would be a good start. There might be a lot of concrete in Thamesmead, but there's earth beneath, but we don't know if that soil is contaminated by the black Dust or not, so we can't trust it. We'll have to import soil, bagged stuff, gro-bags, etc., soil we know is Dust-free."

"Ha, I knew you had the answers!" Charlie slapped his thigh in glee.

"You've really thought this through, haven't you?" Jules said, glowering at Charlie.

"No, not really. I'm just trying to be realistic. We're in a shit situation here, Jules, possibly a no-win situation. I, for one, am never going to accept that. Solutions have to be found, and it's not going to happen overnight. We need to think on it as a group, a democracy, with shared decision making. It's the only way to ensure our survival."

"Then show us the way," said Tina. "Get us through this."

My heart nearly dropped out of my chest. This is not what I intended; I was no leader. I was in no position to accept responsibility for twenty-six souls.

"Now, wait a minute," I said. "I'm not qualified for that. I'll help, even advise, but that's as far as it goes. Jules should be the one since he's the oldest, with advisors making collective decisions for us all after discussing it as a democracy."

The room fell silent.

"Okay, so we become a democracy," said Tom, breaking the awkward quiet. "What do we do next?"

"Nothing," said Jules. "We keep our options open as best we can. Make this place secure and keep our people safe and act as the situation dictates. If, God Forbid, we have to leave, then we'll have to make damned sure we have some-where to go."

"What was that all about?" Jules asked me when we were alone.

"I'm sorry, Jules, but I'm no leader. You already knew that," I said.

"Bullshit, if you'll pardon my French. You're the perfect choice. The others already look up to you. You've got charisma, knowledge..."

"Maybe," I countered, "but it's personal knowledge, and I don't mean that selfishly. In order for me to survive extreme situations, I'm prepared to go to some pretty dire lengths, sometimes bad things, risky even, which makes it a personal choice.

I continued, "Jules, when I go camping, it's not on some safe, registered site where there's toilets and showers and a site shop to buy your bacon and egg breakfast. It's in the wild, often in cold, wet weather. Your next meal depends on what you can snare or hunt, mainly rabbits and sometimes squirrel; or if there's a river or lake, then fish caught with a hand line. Most times you go to sleep hungry and wake up even hungrier. I can't ask these people to accept those conditions."

"I think you'd be surprised," Jules said.

"I can't risk it, especially not with women and children. It would leave me open to mistakes, make me hesitate, and that would be no good for them or me." I continued, "Jesus, Jules, before I came here, I was on my way to Wales or Scotland, anywhere to get me away from here. Now look at me."

"You're a good man, Adam. You got a good heart. You know you're needed here despite your reservations."

"Perhaps, but don't paint me as a saint, Jules; I'm far from that. I'm as scared as the rest of them. Like you said, living from day to day and making it up as I go along. First chance I get when all this is over and done, I'm heading north out of here."

"Of course, you are," Jules said indulgently.

Teresa sat with the boy for two days, hardly leaving his bedside except for brief meal and bathroom breaks. Sally told us that she couldn't hear what Teresa was saying, but it was nonstop. By the afternoon of the second day, the boy seemed to be responding to her, and by that evening, they were holding hands.

"Terry Moore," Teresa said as she stepped out of Sally's front door. "He lived in Dartford."

Tom moved out of his deckchair and offered it to Teresa. She was pale and drawn, dark rings circled her eyes.

"He and his family, his mum, dad, older brother, and younger sister, were going across Dartford Heath after the big storm hit, trying to get to Bluewater for help. His sister, Ellen, was sick. They went through a wooded area when they were attacked. By the way Terry described them, they were Creeps. Only Terry said they were small, no bigger than cats. They ran and got separated. Terry saw his father brought down by a large group of the creatures, all the time he was struggling, his dad yelled at Terry to run. The time from then until Adam found him is hazy. He remembers breaking into shops for food, hiding from people, barricading himself in abandoned houses to sleep. Not much more."

"Christ," said Charlie. "Poor bastard."

"He's safe now," said Jules sombrely. "We'll give him all the care he needs to get past this horror, let him know he's among friends, that we're family."

Everyone nodded except Teresa; she was fast asleep in the deckchair.

"Who's that over there?" I asked Jules the following morning.

It was early, a little past seven. We were in the courtyard having breakfast, enjoying the cool air before it got too hot. The temperature was still rising and didn't look to be stopping anytime soon. Jules looked up from the book he was reading and peered over his glasses to the far corner. A young girl dressed in black leggings and vest top with cropped black hair and covered with tribal tattoos was with Paul Taylor. They looked to be fighting with quarter staffs.

"That's Nat," Jules said, returning to his book. "Natalie Morrison."

I'd seen her about the Block. Until now, I hadn't taken much notice of her. It became obvious she was teaching Paul how to use the quarter staff, showing him some moves.

"She's good," I said.

Jules looked up from his book again. "She trains most days," he said. "Been doing martial arts since she was a kid. She was one of the first people to find me here."

I watched as they switched from the staff to single-sticks. Paul and I watched in amazement as Nat went into an intricate routine designed to demonstrate the versatility of the sticks.

"She's very good," I said.

The throaty roar of motorbikes was loud as they rode under the arch leading into the courtyard. Every head turned to look, and others came out of their flats to see what all the ruckus was about.

Charlie, Tom, and I were seated by one of the fire bins discussing an idea Charlie had about further security for the Block. It wasn't much past 3:00, and there was no fire in the bin, though one had been set earlier. We had acquired a single decker bus and armoured it with some of the heavy mesh and corrugated iron sheets.

It completely blocked the arch, making it impassable. It also gave rise to another problem; once in place, we couldn't see beneath the arch. We solved the problem, or rather Roger Boulton did, by cutting small view ports in the corrugated iron sheets. That in turn raised yet another question.

"I might be overthinking it," said Charlie, "but if we ever did get attacked by Creeps or whatever, we wouldn't be able to see them once they got beneath the arch. And if it was Creeps, when given time, they would wreck the bus and our defences would be breached. What then?"

At first, I considered such a scenario very unlikely, but the world had gone crazy; we'd been invaded by space monkeys and killer plants, so anything was possible.

Then I remembered: *Better to have it and never need it than need it and not have it.*

The solution proved to be simple enough courtesy of Charles Donovan Esquire.

"We rig an oil drum filled with petrol in the middle of the arch against the wall and fix it so a valve opens at the flick of a switch, releasing the petrol. Tom could devise an electrical spark and boom, instant firestorm."

"That's pretty radical, even for you, Charlie. It could easily work against us. It might take the whole Block up with it," I said.

"Not if we moderate the amount of fuel, just enough to discourage incursion. There would be foam extinguishers placed this side of the arch as a precaution. I figure if we ever have to use such measures, we'd be pretty much fucked anyway."

"Well, I can't fault your logic," I said. "Tom?"

The electrician shrugged. "It's a piece of cake, but the trigger for the spark would have to be secured so it's not set off accidently; some of these kids are very inquisitive."

"Absolutely," I agreed. "So, let's get it done…"

That's when the three of us turned around at the sound of motorbikes.

"Jesus Christ!" muttered Charlie. "It's bloody Rambo."

As soon as I saw him, I knew Derek Kaminsky was going to be trouble, and that's before I even knew his name.

Nineteen

May 2018

The three of us got up as the bikers dismounted, kicking down the bike stands and looking around imperiously. Jules came out of his flat, looked at the bikers, across at us, and then started towards our visitors.

Charlie was right; from a distance, the bigger biker was a ringer for Sly Stallone's Rambo. Only from a distance though because as I got closer, the illusion faded. Yeah, he had the shoulder length, curly, black hair held in place by a red bandana. He was big, muscular, and wore a white vest top over faded blue jeans and heavy black boots. I'm not sure if Stallone ever wore Ray-Bans as Rambo, but this guy did, and that's where the similarities ended.

His nose was very prominent, with a lipless mouth that sported a permanent sneer that its owner mistakenly thought looked cool. His left arm was sheathed in a wrist to shoulder tattoo sleeve, but the biggest let down were the eyes. The guy swept off the Ray-Bans in a very affected manner as we converged on him, Jules from the left, the three of us from the right. He regarded us coolly with blue eyes so pale they could have been cataracts. Shockingly, the washed-out colour was accentuated by a deeply tanned face.

The illusion was further shattered as soon as he opened his mouth to speak. It was obvious his crooked, uneven teeth hadn't seen a toothbrush in months, if ever. The broad, Birmingham accent didn't help either.

"Hello and welcome, Gents!" greeted Jules brightly. "What can we do for you?"

"Are you the guy in charge?" he asked.

Jules smiled disarmingly. "No one's in charge here, my friend. We all work for the common good, but you can talk to me. The name's Jules."

Kaminsky ignored Jules' proffered hand as he surveyed the area. I noted the three heavy gold rings on his left hand, two more on his right. The one on his pinkie boasted a formidable ruby. Heavy gold chains adorned both wrists and hung from his thick neck.

"We're just looking for a place to crash for a night or two," the biker said.

"I'm sure we can accommodate you," Jules smiled. "Mr. ...?"

"Kaminsky, Derek Kaminsky," he finally looked at Jules. "This is Pete Hogan." He cocked a thumb at his companion.

Hogan was a lot younger than Kaminsky and didn't seem to fit being with him. I figured Kaminsky was around twenty-eight, maybe a little older. Hogan was no more than twenty-five, fresh faced, light brown hair worn in a pony-tail, blue-eyed, and almost innocent looking. What was he doing with a dick like Kaminsky? He didn't look the syco-phantic type, and he certainly didn't defer to his friend in any way, if friend he was.

"That'd be great, wouldn't it, Pete?" Kaminsky said.

"I could do with a decent night's kip without worrying if I'm gonna wake up being eaten alive," Hogan said.

"You've encountered Creeps then?" Jules asked.

"The furballs? Yeah, we've seen 'em," said Kaminsky without elaborating.

"Where have you come from?"

"All over, recently up from the coast, Margate," Kaminsky said.

"You came up the A2?" Jules asked.

"No, A20, came through Well Hall, stayed at a pub there overnight. Saw your fire glow in the night sky and decided to come and have a look."

"Okay, well, you're welcome to stay for a night or two. Maybe once you get to see what we have here, you might consider joining us. New residents are always welcome."

"Sure," said Kaminsky noncommittally.

Charlie nudged me, nodding at the biker's heavily studded leather belt and the foot long knife hanging from it in an equally heavy leather sheath.

"He's even got the bloody knife," Charlie whispered behind his hand.

"Are you hungry?" Jules asked.

"Yeah, we could eat," Kaminsky said. "Pete?"

"Definitely," Hogan agreed.

"There's stew, mainly vegetable and canned steak, but it's good. And there's fresh baked bread," Jules said.

"Sounds good," said Kaminsky. "I've forgotten what bread tastes like."

Every time he opened his mouth, I disliked him even more.

"Then you're in for a treat," enthused Jules. "It'll be ready in about an hour. You can park your bikes over there by the vans."

"He's lying through his teeth," I said, watching as the two bikers walked their machines across the courtyard and put them next to the vans and my cab.

"Why would you say that?" asked Jules.

"Because if he came up from the A20 through Well Hall, he wouldn't have been able to see our light glow, no matter how bright it was," I said. "You've got Shooters Hill and Red Lion Hill between here and there. It's impossible to have seen anything past those."

"Why would he lie?" asked Tom.

"Did you see the bling he was wearing?" Charlie said. "Gotta wonder where that come from."

"You think they were the looters in Wellingham?" Jules asked.

"I think he went out of his way to make us think he was nowhere near Wellingham. Maybe our friend has a guilty conscience," I said.

"I'm guessing that bike isn't legal either," said Charlie. "What would something like that cost?"

"Thirty, thirty-five thousand," I said. "And it looks brand new."

"You can't blame them for commandeering the bikes," Jules said. "Haven't we been doing the same?"

"Jules is right. Maybe we're being overly suspicious," I said, though my gut was telling me the direct opposite. "We can't judge them out of hand. We will keep an eye on them though, just until we're sure."

As it turned out, it didn't take long for trouble to start.

Sleep has never come easily to me. The only time I sleep well is when I go camping, and then I sleep like the proverbial baby. I was pretty pissed when I was woken up from a deep sleep the following morning by someone banging incessantly on my front door. Bleary-eyed, I answered it to find an agitated Sally looking anxiously over the balcony railing into the courtyard below.

"Adam, you need to come down. It's Roger..."

I could hear raised voices down below, one very threatening. Kaminsky.

"Shit," I swore softly. "Okay Sal, give me a minute."

I threw on some clothes and hurried down to the courtyard. Over by the bikes, a crowd had gathered. Trish Morgan was ushering children away from the altercation, and she threw me a worried look. Pushing through the crowd with quiet apologies, I found Kaminsky towering over Roger Boulton. Overweight and about six inches shorter, Roger was no match for the biker, but he wasn't backing down.

"I was just looking," Roger was saying. "I was nowhere near the bloody panniers."

"What else you gonna say?" snarled Kaminsky. "You better hope nothing's missing."

"Nothing will be," I said, stepping between the two men. "What's going on here?"

"Ask your man here, sticking his nose in where it don't belong," Kaminsky said.

"I was just looking, Adam," said Roger. "It's a Honda Goldwing, eighteen-thirty-three c.c, six-cylinder, seven-speed automatic. A dream on wheels."

"Yeah, my dream," Kaminsky said.

"He's a mechanic," I said, referring to Roger. "Cars, bikes, anything mechanical, it's his passion, a total nerd. If he's caused offence, it was unintended, and I'm sure he's sorry."

"Sure," agreed Roger.

Kaminsky looked from me to Roger; he didn't look placated. Then Pete Hogan appeared on the scene, and in a split second, Kaminsky's attitude did a strange U-turn.

"You know what?" he suddenly said, his hands outspread. "Maybe I did overreact. It's been a tough time for us all." He turned to Roger and clapped a friendly hand on his shoulder. "I'm sorry, man. I didn't mean to go all ballistic."

Roger was surprised; words wouldn't come.

"You're right. My bike is a dream on wheels, and it ought to be appreciated," Kaminsky said.

"Yeah," Roger stammered. "Yeah…"

"No hard feelings." Kaminsky smiled.

Kaminsky's expression reminded me of a shark.

"Did I miss something?" Roger said after Kaminsky had gone back to the flat allocated to him, closely followed by Hogan. "I was just looking, Adam. Professional interest. He acted as if I was going to steal the bloody thing."

"It's okay, Roger," I said. "Like he said, just a little bit of overreaction. Forget it."

"Now that was weird," said Charlie. "I thought it was gonna get physical for sure."

"That was never going to happen," I said, "but you're right, it was weird. He turned on a sixpence."

"It was a storm in a teacup," Jules said. "We've all been under a lot of strain lately and can you wonder at it? There's a lot of tension in the air."

"Yeah, yeah, you're probably right, Jules," I said.

Bullshit, I thought.

Later that day, I watched the two bikers roar out of the courtyard.

"Are they coming back?" I asked Jules, who had been talking to them just before they left.

"I think so," he said. "I told them the arch is closed at sundown. Derek said they just needed some air."

The van door slamming shut diverted my attention. Alan Holden and Jeff Shepherd were preparing to go out on another one of their forays. Both men, unattached and with no dependants, had taken it on themselves to become our scavengers, trawling the area in their van looking mainly for food but on the lookout for anything else that might be of use.

"Excuse me, Jules," I said and hurried over to the van. "Alan, a word?"

He regarded me quizzically.

"Where are you going today?" I asked.

"We thought towards Dartford. There's a couple of industrial estates out there we want to check out."

"Could you keep an eye out for something for me?" I asked.

"Sure. Name it," he said amiably.

I told him and he laughed. "Really?"

"Absolutely," I answered. "That okay?"

"We'll see what we can do," he said, still laughing as he and Jeff got into the van and pulled out.

I'd been thinking of my encounter with the Creeps in Park Vista Road for some time. I couldn't explain their uncanny behaviour, but I believed I knew why they had gathered there, watching me. Noise. The sound of my cab had attracted them. I don't know why I hadn't realised that before; it was that obvious.

I had noticed signs of rabbits in the soft mud, mainly droppings, slightly larger than before, but definitely rabbits. Denford Park had also been teeming with squirrels before the troubles. *Is that still the case? Do the Creeps hunt other animals for prey?* One would assume so; I intended to find out. The thought of fresh meat was beginning to haunt me: sausages, bacon, roast lamb. I was craving it more and more.

I was confident I could bag either or both rabbits and squirrels. Hunting or trapping, I was pretty good at both skills. They made good eating and were a thousand times better than canned steak, corned beef, and hotdogs. But this wasn't the uplands of Scotland. Up there you weren't being hunted as you were hunting. It would take patience, and there was the danger. The Creeps didn't seem to like leaving the shelter of the woods, though I had to wonder how long that would last. They were evolving, getting bigger; they were definitely getting bigger. Terry said those that attacked him were no larger than cats, and the ones I saw were as big as chimpanzees. One on one, I didn't think I would stand much of a chance.

If I was quiet, kept it on the downlow, there was no reason I shouldn't try my luck. The thought of barbequed rabbit flooded my mouth with juices. Once decided, I spent the rest of the day making snares, thinking I'd use every resource possible. It was worth the try.

Commotion within the Block usually meant trouble. The continual blaring of the car horn brought everyone running, me included. Only it wasn't a car; it was Alan and Jeff returning from their foraging in a very excited manner, yelling and shouting, gathering everyone to them.

"You won't believe it!" Alan was yelling. "It's bloody incredible!"

Jeff was at the rear of the van, equally excited. He saw me crossing the courtyard. I was coming to stand beside Jules and Sally. Both had eager expressions on their faces, infected by the two men's enthusiasm.

"Adam!" called Jeff. "This is amazing. You gotta see this!"

"We found a farm," Alan said, the words spilling from his mouth. "Just past Ruxley Corner. The place was not overgrown; the vines barely had a hold. We decided to chance it and checked the house and outbuildings.

"There was this silo; noises were coming from inside. Jeff was all for leaving, but then we heard sounds that we just knew were not Creeps."

"Okay, okay, you got us hooked," laughed Jules. "What the hell was it?"

Alan nodded at Jeff to reach into the rear of the van. There was a bit of a scuffle, and then he stepped back and came out with a chicken cradled in his arms! There were audible gasps as the chicken's head bobbed left and right, taking in its new surroundings.

"Bloody hell, that's a big 'un!" whistled Charlie. "That's gotta be three times its normal size!"

More clucking came from inside the van as we all pushed forward to peer inside, the children squealing with delight.

"There's four of 'em," said Alan. "There were others, but they were dead. I think they weren't strong enough to survive."

"How the hell have they managed to survive this long?" I asked, dumbfounded.

"The silo," said Alan. "It was full of grain. They'd been feeding off that, and there was a tap dripping in the barn, filling a bucket.

"There's more..." Alan said, sliding open the van's side door and hefting out a wooden crate and putting it on the ground.

"Eggs!" Sally gasped. "Big eggs. They're as big as cricket balls!"

"We loaded three crates and brought them back," explained Jeff. "We didn't know if they would be any good, but they were too good an opportunity to leave behind."

"Someone get a bucket of water," I said, picking up one of the eggs. It must have weighed over a pound.

"The water test," said Sally.

"Yep," I agreed.

"Water test?" Charlie said, puzzled.

"If you drop an egg into water," Sally explained, "and it floats, it's no good to eat. If it sinks and lays flat on the bottom, then it's fresh. If they are a week or so old, it will sink and stand on one end, but it's still safe to eat."

"Then let's get that bucket!" Charlie said.

There were twenty-seven eggs. Nine were fresh, sixteen were a week or so old, and two we weren't sure about, so they were discarded. It was amazing, a spectacular find, and it sent the morale within the Block into the stratosphere.

"Where are we going to put them?" asked Trish Morgan, looking at the chickens.

"In the corner, over there," said Jules. "We'll build a holding pen and a coop, and you and the children can help look after them. What d'you think?"

Trish was beaming. "That's a wonderful idea. I could work out a rota, involve all the youngsters."

I could see Trish's mind already working as she fussed the chicken still in Jeff's arms. So was Sally's as she avariciously eyed the eggs.

"Tonight we celebrate," she announced. "Eggs for everyone: omelettes, fried, scrambled... your choice!"

That raised a cheer.

They were still cheering when Alan pulled me aside.

"We didn't forget you." He grinned.

Jeff was clambering on the van's roof rack, pulling aside a tarpaulin. He lowered my prize down to Alan.

"A pushbike," Charlie said, giving Alan a hand.

"Absolutely," I said.

"We found a Halfords," Alan said. "There were dozens of bikes there, but I figured this one would suit best, offroader, five speed gears, sprung front forks."

The shining blue machine looked great, ideal for my purposes. Now I could roam the area in silence, go hunting, get near to the edges of woodlands with the minimum of danger.

"We got these, too," Alan said, producing another crate from the van containing four spare inner tubes, a pump, a puncture repair kit, and some other stuff. There were also spare tyres. "If you need anything else just let us know and we'll pick it up for you.

"We're going back to the farm tomorrow with some sacks and salvage some of that grain to keep the chickens happy."

It had been a good day. Not even Kaminsky's return dampened the jovial atmosphere. It was really good was seeing Terry Moore sitting outside of Sally's with a blanket over his shoulders tucking into a plate of scrambled eggs. He was given first dibs by Sally as an incentive to leave his sick bed.

It was a pleasure quietly watching the happy faces in the gentle glow of the fires, talking, laughing, happy. Charlie was still tucking into egg sandwiches and drinking a beer while playing the fool to his kids as Julie laughed at his antics. Nat and Paul were talking, probably about martial arts, though I hoped it was something a little more intimate; they were sitting very close to one another.

Alan and Jeff's conversation was heard by everyone. They were sitting with Andrew Taylor, laughing loudly at the afternoon escapades with the chickens. After the furor over the chickens' arrival had died down, Jules suggested they temporarily put the birds in one of the few remaining flats till the coop could be built. It turned out to be easier said than done. Two of the oversized chickens escaped. They were trapped within the courtyard and had nowhere to go, but it didn't stop them running amok. Jeff, Alan, and Charlie were led a merry dance trying to catch them, resulting in shrieking laughter from the children and adults alike.

Some of the others joined in the great chicken hunt, finally cornering the wayward birds and forcing them into the flat. Everyone started cheering as Charlie and company took their bows at a job well done. When Sally and Trish Morgan announced that the first batch of eggs was ready, the cheering started again. Plates in hand, a line quickly formed outside Sally's front door as all eagerly awaited a rare treat. As promised, there were omelettes, scrambled, and fried eggs. It was a feast indeed with many, including me, going back for seconds.

"May I?" Tina Mitchell indicated the chair next to mine.

"Of course," I said, a little startled. "Everything okay?"

"It's fine. The twins are asleep, so I'm grabbing a little free time while I can. It's been an eventful day."

"It has—a good day," I said, echoing my earlier thoughts.

"Except for the scene this morning," Tina said. "Is Roger okay? I haven't had a chance to speak to him yet."

"He's good. As Jules said, it was just a storm in a teacup, done and dusted."

"Good, I'm glad. Rodger's a good man," she said.

Silence hung between us for a few moments as we watched the others in the ruddy glow of the fires.

"Tell me about this camping you do," Tina suddenly said.

"What d'you want to know?" I answered.

"What do you do out there in the wild all by yourself? Doesn't it get lonely?"

I chuckled. "Everybody asks that. The truth is I'm alone, not lonely. There's a difference. You don't have time to get lonely. It's a bit more than sitting around a campfire frying sausages and swigging beer, though that does come into it."

It was good to hear her laugh.

"Isn't it dangerous?" she asked.

"Not really, not if you know what you're doing. Of course, there's plenty of would-be survivalists out there who really haven't got a clue. They're really just armchair campers, except for the glampers."

"Glampers?" she queried, and I laughed.

"Glamorous camping, where everything is laid on, no effort involved, like going to a hotel in the woods."

"Seems like more my style." She laughed.

"Enough of me. What about you? How are you holding up? I sometimes saw you in Buckingham Avenue…"

"Yeah, I loved that house," Tina said wistfully. She fell quiet.

"What about family?" I asked, changing the subject.

"Well, I have two sisters who live in Downham. Mum and Dad are in Bermondsey, or at least they were. God alone knows what's happened to them now. Then there's me and the twins." She paused, considering. "I was married. Guess I still am, but he left six months after Mark and Matthew were born, obviously not cut out for fatherhood and married life."

"I'm sorry. It must have been hard," I sympathised.

"It was at first, but that was a long time ago." She smiled wanly. "Have you any family?"

"Nope, just me," I said. "Until now."

She looked at me puzzled and then smiled.

"Oh," she said, getting it, "this lot."

"I never thought in a million years I'd end up in a situation like this; life certainly can throw some curves at us. If someone had told me a year ago that I'd be living in sheltered accommodation with a bunch of strangers, I would have told them they're crazy. Who can say where we'll end up?"

"That's been on my mind a lot lately," Tina said, frowning. "Where are we going to end up? My babies, all the other kids? It doesn't bear thinking about."

"Hey, it'll be all right. We'll find a way through this together," I said. "We just have to keep positive."

"I try," Tina said, "but it's hard sometimes. You help me a lot."

"Me?" I said, surprised.

"Yeah, you always seem to have an answer. It gives me and a lot of others confidence."

"Tina, I'm just winging it, Love. Taking it day by day."

A burst of laughter broke the sombre mood.

"Hark at me," Tina said. "The last thing you need is a wet blanket spoiling the day."

"It's all right," I comforted. "It's hard for all of us. Maybe that's our strength. At least now I have something to make me smile if things get bleak: Charlie being knocked on his arse by a two-foot, rampaging chicken!"

We laughed.

"That was funny!" Tina giggled. "The look on his face! How on earth did they get so big?"

"No idea," I answered. "Obviously something to do with the black Dust and the rain. Just another mystery we'll probably never know the answer to."

"Puts a whole new slant on chicken wings!" Tina started laughing again.

"And chicken drumsticks!"

We sat quietly enjoying each other's company. Two strangers in an oasis of light in a dark empty city, watching cold, bright stars in the clear night sky that didn't give a damn about what was happening below them.

"I was thinking," Tina said in a low voice, "would you like to come to dinner tomorrow night? I'm getting a little tired of all the communal meals and ... well, I wanted something a little more normal. Something a little more intimate and friendly, soft music and a glass of wine."

I looked at her. She was quiet, unassuming, but there was something below the surface that spoke to me. She was an attractive woman, long, sandy hair cascading over her shoulders and down her back, soft brown eyes. There was a self-reliance in the way she held herself, a quiet determination. Something stirred inside me; it made me feel good. Here, I knew I could have a good friend, a true friend. Something we would all need in the crazy, upside-down world we were now living in.

"Yes," I said, "I'd like that."

"Obviously nothing fancy," she smiled, "but I can cook."

"Never doubted it," I said. "I'll bring the wine, red and white."

"Okay, about eight?"

I nodded.

She stood up. "I'd better get back to the twins. Good night, Adam."

"Night, Tina."

Quietly, she slipped away into the shadows.

Twenty

November 2018

Being out on the bike for the first time was weird. The rifle was slung across my back, the Glock on my left hip, my knife on the right, and my pouch in the small of my back. I must have looked strange, dare I say funny, armed to the teeth, riding a bright blue push-bike through the deserted streets of Wellingham.

Feelings of vulnerability nagged at my mind, but I wasn't scared. It was sort of exhilarating, and I noticed a lot more of my surroundings than I would have behind the wheel of the cab. Sweat sheathed my body as the temperature rose. Each day seemed to be hotter than the last, forcing me to wear a cap, which I hated, and long-sleeved cotton shirts. The sun was fierce, and as much as I loved it, it was getting just a little too hot.

I made light of the weather back at the Block. Just an Indian summer—England gets them now and then. From the looks I got in response, I knew that you could only fool the people some of the time.

From the cover of some cars, I scanned the line of Oaks bordering the park where I had seen the Creeps gathering last time. Testing theories can be dangerous, and coming out here on a push-bike was one of those theories. But it paid off. The binoculars showed no sign of the Creeps in the trees. I cycled a little closer to make sure the trees were empty. Taking the opportunity, I examined the soft ground near the wrought iron fencing; it was littered with rabbit droppings. Keeping clear of the rustling vines, I followed the droppings to the right till I came to a chain link fence. Most of the rabbit activity seemed to be in this area.

"As good a place as any," I said as I dumped a can of sweet corn taken from my backpack, scattering it where there was the most sign.

Satisfied, I remounted and headed for north Wellingham to see what I could find. It was a pleasant day riding through the town, mentally marking where the vines were gaining ground, amazed at the speed with which they grew. I was convinced it was only a matter of time before we would seriously have to consider relocating.

Lunch was egg sandwiches eaten in the welcoming shade of a bus stop. It had me wondering how long it would be before I grew tired of eggs. Scanning the streets with the binoculars while I ate, I was hoping to see some sign of life, but there was nothing. No smoke, no noise. Exactly what I was hoping to find I wasn't sure, but something, anything. Perhaps it was just a need to find someone out here, the possibility of hope rekindled. I was disappointed.

When I returned to the Block, Tom Taylor, Charlie, Roger, and Stephen were busy building a chicken coop in the corner of the courtyard using left over steel mesh and two by four timbers. A plywood coop was constructed into the corner.

"Looking good, boys!" I called as I parked my bike at the foot of the stairs.

"This is the easy part," Roger called back, wiping the sweat from his face with a big red handkerchief. "Getting the chickens into it is gonna be something else."

"Get Charlie to do it," I joked. "He's got the experience."

"Har, har, har," Charlie retorted.

"Seriously, if you want to make it easy, move 'em at night. Keep the lights off in the flat, and you'll be able to just pick the chickens up. The darkness makes them docile, so they won't resist or struggle, I promise," I advised.

The knock on the door was hesitant, almost timid. Terry Moore stood on the balcony, shuffling from one foot to the other, looking very awkward.

"Hey, Terry. How you doing?" I asked brightly.

"I'm good," he said, looking around nervously.

"Come in, come in. What can I do for you?"

"No, no, I won't come in," he said, actually taking a step back as if he thought I might attack him. "I just came to thank you for helping me."

"Well, that's no problem, but you don't have to thank me. I'm just glad I was there to help."

"I do have to thank you. It's only right." He was becoming agitated, biting his lower lip.

"Okay. I appreciate you coming to tell me," I said. "Is there anything else you need?"

"No, Sally's looking after me real good." He started to walk away then stopped. "Thanks again."

Turning abruptly, Terry hurriedly walked off. I watched him disappear down the stairs. He never looked back once. The experience with the Creeps had marked him. I've no idea how he was before the attack, but I was pretty sure it wasn't like this. I hoped time would help him forget, and if there was anyone here that could help him, it would be Sally. I hoped so anyway. I hadn't even thought about Teresa helping him at that point. Sometimes you just don't see the obvious.

After showering, I stood in the bedroom with a towel around my waist, trying to decide what to wear. I couldn't believe how nervous I was; it was like I was seventeen again going out on a first date. Jenny West, what a disaster that was. In the end, I just wore a clean pair of jeans and a shirt.

The courtyard was aglow as I made my way around the balcony to the stairs on the farther side just before eight. Trish had her kids seated around one of the oil drum fires. Toasting marshmallows on long sticks, they were giggling and enjoying the new experience. Aided by Joan Peoples, Trish was doing a good job as a surrogate mother. They started as her pupils, but now they were her children. The teacher turned mother.

Tina was waiting by her open front door.

"Good evening," I said.

She smiled and ushered me in. "I don't want to wake the twins," she said quietly, closing the door.

"You look lovely," I said, admiring the simple white blouse and dark blue skirt, "and dinner smells great."

She blushed. "Thank you. Come on. Let's sit down. Dinner won't be long."

The room was dimly lit. Soft music, Pachelbel, was playing in the background.

"Wine," I said, proffering the bottles.

It was a wonderful evening. Dinner was homemade steak pie with canned potatoes and peas as sides, though you wouldn't have known it. Desert was peach cobbler, which went well with the Chardonnay. I didn't know if that was wine etiquette, but I liked it.

"So, there you are deep in the woods in the middle of nowhere, it's pitch black, and you hear a rustling outside your tent. What do you do?" she asked.

We were sitting on the sofa drinking wine by candlelight.

"Probably turn over and go back to sleep," I said.

"Never!" She laughed. "You wouldn't be scared?"

"Of what? A fox rummaging around the ashes from the fire? A curious badger?" I asked. "There's no predatory animals left in the U.K., and I don't believe in Big Foot."

"What if it was an escaped lunatic?" Tina persisted.

"In the middle of nowhere? I don't think so."

"I'd be terrified."

"No, you wouldn't. You'd be perfectly safe," I said.

"Perhaps, but it's not so safe out there now."

"Mmmmm... I was thinking that too."

"Does it make you sad?" she asked.

"That I might never be able to camp out in the woods again or visit wild places? Absolutely."

"I'm sorry."

"As if it's your fault. No, it'll work out. Somehow, some way, we'll figure a way to get rid of the vines and the Creeps. I'm pretty sure the authorities are already working on the problem."

"You really think so?"

"Like Jules said, we have to believe in something. The trick is to stay alive till it happens."

"I wish I had done and seen the things you have; it must be wonderful. When Brian, my husband, left, I wondered for a long time what I had done wrong. I thought it was all my fault. For a while, I regretted having the twins, and I know that sounds awful. I believed that my life was over and that I had taken the wrong path. I didn't want to see family; I didn't want to see friends. For the longest time it was just me and the twins. Then I realised they were my whole world."

Tina went on, "I missed out on a lot of things, lost a lot of friends, till my sisters declared enough was enough. They showed me I wasn't to blame, it wasn't my fault, and I started to come out of my shell, began living again. They literally pulled me back into the world." She laughed. "Now look at us."

"It isn't always wine and roses being on your own," I said. "For the most part, I've been happy with my life. I just have a problem with people in the long term. A natural loner, I guess. All our lives have been changed, turned upside down. We have to change with them, learn to adapt, and make the most of it."

"You make it sound so easy."

"It's never going to be easy, but if we stick together, watch out for each other, we can get past this and start to rebuild what we had, for us and the kids."

The oil drum fires were burning low, the ruddy light failing. The wine had gone to my head, and I realised I was talking too much. I couldn't remember the last time I had done that.

"It's getting late. I should go," I said. "I've had a lovely evening."

"Then stay."

I wasn't sure my befuddled brain had heard her correctly, but I didn't make any effort to get off the sofa.

"Maybe a little longer." I smiled.

"No, I meant stay."

The next thing I knew she was in my arms, kissing me. I resisted for about a second, and then we were kissing each other. Laying back, she drew me down onto the sofa, her lips soft on mine, her hands pulling urgently at my clothes and squeezing my shoulders. Then the floodgates opened, and we were tearing at each other's clothes, scrabbling with buttons, touching, kissing, wanting.

I woke, my head muzzy, my mouth sticky and dry. It was early; grey light filtered through the curtains. I had no idea how I had gotten home. I didn't remember leaving Tina's. Then I realised, I wasn't home. This wasn't my bedroom. Suddenly wide awake, I looked beside me. Tina lay there, her hair cascading over the pillow, a serene contentment written on her face. Lying back into the pillows, I silently cursed the wine. I hadn't meant for this to happen, but I immediately knew that was a lie. I had wanted something to happen; I just hadn't thought it through. Now I had created a situation that could be embarrassing for both of us.

I slipped out of bed and silently gathered my clothes. Finding my shirt still in the living room, I dressed quickly. Thankfully, the twins still slept as I opened the front door, wincing when it closed with a loud "click." The morning was already warm, though the sun had barely risen as I took the stairs two at a time back up to the balcony. Swiftly getting home, I let myself in, leaning back on the door with relief.

I didn't know what last night had meant, if it meant anything at all, but the memory of it had me smiling. We were adults and would treat it as adults, but I kept thinking I had taken things too far. Tina was vulnerable, and I feared I had taken advantage of her vulnerability.

"Damn…" I muttered.

I didn't know it then, but as stealthy as I had been, hostile eyes had seen me leaving Tina's place. There was no way I could have anticipated the terrible consequences discovery would bring.

Restless now, I showered, brushed the dryness out of my mouth, threw on some clean clothes, and headed out. The Block was already stirring as I walked my bike towards the arch. Roger had already moved the bus in anticipation of Alan and Jeff going on one of their forays. He waved when he saw me.

"You're early."

"Thought I'd make the most of the morning before it gets too hot," I said.

"Good idea," he agreed. "Oh, by the way, it worked."

"Worked?"

"Yeah, moving the chickens. We did as you said and turned off the lights. The chickens didn't so much as twitch a muscle. We got them all in the coop without a hitch."

I laughed. "Glad to hear it, though it might have been good to see Charlie chasing them all over the place again."

"It would," he agreed. "Charlie said something about you being a David Attenborough. Not sure what that meant."

"Don't worry, Roger. I do. I'll see you later."

Using some shopping carts and green curtains I found in a nearby haberdashery shop, I fashioned a crude hide close to where I had left the corn. I had already ascertained that yesterday's corn had been eaten and laid a fresh tin. Creating a shelter against the sun, I settled down to wait. Three hours later and still nothing. Eventually it got too hot to stay any longer, so I decided to try again tomorrow.

As I parked my bike, Joan Peoples intercepted me as I mounted the stairs. She had a notebook in her hand and a strange look on her face.

"Joan?" I queried.

"I need to speak with you about the stores," she said brusquely.

Joan, always with a matter-of-fact attitude, seemed to be even more earnest now. She was painfully thin, had serious brown eyes, and had prematurely grey hair that tended to the frizzy side which she wore it in a tight bun at the back of her narrow head. She reminded me of a school-teacher I had in primary school.

"What about them?" I asked.

"Someone's stealing them. I wasn't sure at first," she said, pushing her thick rimmed glasses back up her aquiline nose as she flipped open her notebook. "But the stores don't match my list. There's six tins of steak missing, four cans of corned beef, eight of baked beans and six of hotdogs, all unaccounted for."

"Have you spoken to Jules about this?" I asked.

"Yes, we've both been keeping an eye on the flats containing the stores, but whoever is stealing them is clever; they seem to know when the stores aren't being watched, which means they are probably being stolen during the night. Jules and I thought that perhaps we should start locking the stores."

"No, that's not a good idea," I cut in. "The food is communal. Everyone has a right of access."

"I agree, but we still need to keep a check on supplies. No one is saying that people shouldn't have the food. Just mark off what you are taking on the clipboards provided."

"Okay, there's a communal meeting in a couple of days. We'll address the problem then. Make sure people follow the prescribed procedures. Okay?"

"That would be a help. Thank you."

"No problem, Joan. Enjoy the rest of your day."

Tina was waiting for me outside my door. My mind blanked, not sure what to expect. She looked at me, expressionless. "I missed you this morning."

"I know. I'm sorry, but I was thinking of the twins," I lied. "I didn't think it would be a good thing them seeing me in their home so early in the morning."

"Oh," she said, "a goodbye would have been nice."

"You looked so peaceful; I didn't want to wake you up."

"Do you regret last night?" she asked bluntly.

"God, no! I had a great time! It's just ... maybe I overstepped the mark. I didn't mean it to go as far as it did."

"I did," she said. "I think it's what we both needed."

I was lost for words. Suddenly she laughed, mischief shining in her eyes.

"Relax, Adam. It is what it is. I won't be expecting you to make an honest woman out of me. It was a bit of fun. Nothing more."

The look of relief on my face must have been obvious because she said, "Of course, that's not to say it has to be a one off."

Still laughing, she kissed me quickly on the cheek. "I think you're lovely," she said, and with a knowing wink, she skipped lightly down the stairs.

As night began to fall, the fires were lit, and most of the residents gathered in the courtyard. Roger Boulton had fashioned a barbeque out of an old oil drum cut lengthways, bolted to a metal framework for legs.

"Magic," Charlie said sarcastically. "Now all we need is some steak and we can make kebabs."

"Not steak," said Sally as she and Julie appeared, carrying two covered trays.

They set them down on a table, and Julie whipped off the cloths.

"Homemade hamburgers."

The children squealed with delight.

"Sally, you're a marvel!" Roger said.

"Not me. Julie. I only helped," said Sally.

"So, you're keeping secrets now, Mrs. Donovan!" Charlie said. "They look great!"

"Thank Jeff and Alan. They found the canned minced meat. I just added a few bits to make them more palatable."

"A joint effort all round," Jules said happily. "I'll do my part and eat 'em! Let's get grilling!"

Fresh baked buns, burgers, canned onions, barbequed beans, and tinned hot dogs for those who wanted them. Magic, to paraphrase Charlie.

I laid in the next morning instead of getting up with the lark. Last night's barbeque had only heightened my craving for fresh meat, and I was determined to get some. I hadn't had any luck with my early morning hunting, so I decided to change tactics and try later on in the day around mid-afternoon, a couple of hours before dusk.

A leisurely shower and shave followed by a quiet breakfast of bread and strawberry jam with two cups of tea took up most of the morning. I dressed, gathered my gear, and went down to my bike.

"Uncle Adam, whatcha doing?"

Juney came rushing over and launched herself into my arms, closely followed by her brother.

"Good morning little 'un!" I said, hugging her. "I'm just going out for a while. What are you up to?"

"Nothing much," she said as I put her down.

"I bet he's going hunting for rabbits," David said, looking at the rifle slung on my bike. "That's what Dad says."

"Does he now?" I said, ruffling his hair. "Maybe."

"You don't hurt them do you, Uncle Adam?" The distraught look on her face was so sweet.

"Of course not, my Lovely," I said. "This is a special rifle, a quiet rifle. It doesn't make a loud noise, so the rabbits don't hear it and feel no pain."

"And then we get to eat them," David said enthusiastically.

"Yeah, there is that, you bloodthirsty pirate."

"Good morning all, what's going on here then?" Charlie said, munching on one of yesterday's hamburgers.

"Uncle Adam's going hunting with a quiet gun," Juney informed him. "Promises not to hurt the rabbits."

Charlie's eyebrows rose at this snippet of information. "Really? Wow, that's really good. Now go on you two. Mum's got lunch ready, and then you got lessons with Trish."

The children's faces fell.

"Aw dad..." they choroused.

"Get on with you!" Charlie said good-naturedly as they scampered off. "Quiet gun?" he said, turning back to me.

"Yeah," I said. "I figured they've seen enough bad stuff. They don't need to think of anymore."

"Definitely," Charlie agreed. "Well, good luck with that. I'll see you later."

He followed after his children.

"I'll give David Attenborough your regards!" I shouted.

Charlie laughed and gave me the finger.

Cycling beneath the arch, little did I know that I would have a rendezvous that day with three plump rabbits and three savage dogs...

Twenty-One

November 2018
THAMESMEAD

"Eighteen years I've lived here," Jules said. "We moved here just after my Celeste was diagnosed with cancer. She was a strong woman. It broke my heart to see her fade away before my eyes and not be able to do a damn thing about it. She needed help, more than I could give her, so we gave up our home and the garden she loved and moved here into sheltered housing. Three years, fighting tooth and nail, never complaining … and then she passed."

"How long were you married?" I asked.

"Twenty-seven wonderful years. We had two sons, Raymond, the eldest and Julian. Raymond is a career soldier; he's a major now. The last I heard he was in Iraq training their security forces. Julian married an American girl and moved to Texas. Gave us two lovely grandchildren."

"You must be proud of them," I said.

"More than proud." He looked wistfully at the skyline. "I hope they're okay."

The London landscape sprawled out before us as we watched in comfortable silence. The Block's rooftop had become a sort of private sanctum where I could go to think and sometimes talk things out with Jules. It was too hot to come up here through the day; the concrete roof was uncomfortable to walk on even when wearing shoes. I had brought a large beach umbrella up with a patio table and chairs, affording some shade in the twilight hours when the heat was less but still hot enough to raise a sweat.

"The meeting will be starting soon. We should go down," Jules said.

"Give it a few minutes," I replied.

"Still having doubts?" Jules asked.

"I don't know if I'm ready for the responsibility," I said. "It's only been ten months, and we're having to relocate already. Even starting over in another place, who's to say when that place becomes unsafe?"

"We have to let the future take care of itself, go with what we know. The Block has been good to us, but now it's becoming untenable."

"I get that," I said. "I just keep having a recurring fear that eventually nowhere is going to be safe, that we will run out of options."

"There's no way we can pre-empt circumstances or plan for the unknown. We can only do the best we can. The responsibility does not rest with you alone. That's why we made everything a joint decision, so everybody knows exactly what's going on and can have a say."

The clouds began to break up and the sun broke through; the heat went up several notches.

"Come on," I sighed. "Let's get this done."

Several large beach umbrellas had been erected in the courtyard, echoing the rooftop sanctum, vivid splashes of colour that belayed the seriousness of the moment. Coolers loaded with drinks were available. Sally handed Jules a clipboard as we came down the stairs, and everyone falling silent as he took his place at the table placed in front of the assembly.

"Good afternoon," he began. "I'm glad you all could make it. It's a good turn out."

A ripple of laughter flowed over the gathering.

"Okay, let's begin. There's a couple of points I'd like to deal with first, if that's all right. Firstly, I'd like to publicly thank Jeff and Alan for their continued efforts in scavenging for us, notably the laptops and educational software for Trish and the children, much appreciated. Also, I think we can show our appreciation for the chickens, except maybe Charlie."

The laughter was louder this time.

"Joan has brought to my attention that food is being taken from the stores without being signed out. This may sound like a trivial thing, but Joan works hard to ensure there are adequate supplies available at all times; come on, people. The food is yours. It only takes a few seconds to sign it out, so let's make Joan's job as easy as possible."

Jules paused to take a sip of water before continuing, "I mentioned Trish earlier, and I think she deserves a show of thanks for selflessly educating our children. As does Joan, who frequently assists Trish; both work extremely hard in very difficult circumstances."

The applause was spontaneous and heartfelt, making both women blush profusely. Jules waited till the clapping stopped before going on.

"Now we come to the main order of business. We all know the situation, so I don't need to go into that. We all know that the situation is subject to change, and I'm afraid the time for change is now. I'm going to get Adam up here and he'll explain further. Adam…"

Taking a deep breath, I stepped forward as Jules sat down amidst quiet murmurings.

"Thanks Jules," I began, all eyes on me. "Okay, this is how it is. I've been out in the local area several times, as have Jeff, Alan, and Tom. We've observed and noted the continual changes, and it's not good. I'm not going to pull any punches here. You need to know the facts, so we can reach a mutually agreed solution. The vines are growing exponentially at an incredible rate. Earlier this week I passed Buckingham Avenue; it's gone, inundated with vines, so is Denford Park and many of the surrounding streets. I got a map of the area and have begun marking off the vines' advance. Based on information received and personally observed, I think we are safe for the moment. Give it six months, maybe less, we are going to be completely surrounded by a jungle of vines."

The alarmed expressions were immediate.

"I know, I know," I continued. "There are those of you who think we could defend the Block, but we need to look at the bigger picture. At the moment, we have a ton of supplies and water, but both commodities are finite. What do we do when the supplies run out? We have Blackheath and Greenwich Park to the north. Plumstead and Woolwich Commons to the east. Denford Park, Oxleas Wood, and Crown Woods to the west, and acres of open farmland and woods to the south. On a wider scale, we are already pretty much hemmed in."

"So what are we going to do?" asked Tom.

"In my view, the only thing we can do: relocate," I said.

"To where?" Tina asked. "Where can we go that there are no parks or woodlands?"

"We have had some informal discussion on the subject," I said. "Jules, Jeff, Alan, and myself feel our options are obviously somewhat limited, and the only place that may possibly suit our needs is Thamesmead. It's renowned for being mostly concrete, industrial, and that may be our best defence."

"How do we know it's going to be any safer there?" asked Julie.

"We don't," I said. "That's why it needs to be checked out before we commit ourselves."

"You intend to go there and see what the conditions are?" asked Tina.

"Exactly, which is the second part of our agenda today. I propose to go to Thamesmead, check it out, and confirm it's a viable option to relocate."

"You mean you're going on your own?" Tina asked.

"I'm the obvious choice," I said. "I know the area. I know London, every back street."

"That's not going to happen," said Charlie. "Going out there on your own is suicide."

"I've been doing exactly that for the last eight months," I said. "I can travel light, fast, and I haven't any dependants."

"Fuck dependants!" snapped Charlie. "We're all family here now. We work together; isn't that what you said? If you're going, I'm going with you."

"No, you're not. You have Julie and the kids to think about."

"Which is all the more reason I should go," argued Charlie. "They're my family, and I've got every right to protect and do what's best for them, or what sort of man does that make me?"

"A husband and a father," I said.

"And what if, God Forbid, anything should happen to you?" Julie put in. "How does that help us, not knowing if you're alive or not? You need someone to go with you so you can watch each other's back."

"I'll go, too," Jeff said, standing up.

"And me!" Alan said. "Me and Jeff are used to being out there. We know what to expect."

"I want to go too!" Andrew Taylor said.

"Now hold on," I said. "As much as I appreciate the support, this is the very reason I should go alone; you all have families." I looked at Jeff and Alan. "And your contributions to the Block are far too valuable. They need you here."

"If that's your only argument, then none of us should go," Sally put in. "As Charlie said, we are all family now, we stick together, through fair weather and foul. If one is threatened, then we are all threatened, and we face it together."

The clanging of an oil drum silenced the argument. Jules stood with a length of wood, looking from person to person.

"This isn't going to solve anything," he said in a low voice that everybody heard. "The fact is we can't stay here, and Thamesmead is the only viable option; making sure it's safe is imperative. We can't all go and reconnoitre the area, so I suggest we elect three people to be our scouts. Adam is one, Charlie is two, we need a third."

"I'll go." Natalie Morrison stood up. "I can look after myself, I can handle living rough, and the women need to be represented." She winked at me. "Can't let the men have all the fun."

"You tell 'em, girl!" Tina shouted, pumping the air with a fist. Most of the other women agreed.

"That's not a good idea," I said.

"Really? You're going to play the *you're a woman* card?" Nat said. "I tell you what: if you can put me down, I'll stay. What do you say?"

I was hopelessly outgunned.

"Okay," said Jules. "It's decided. Adam, Charlie, and Nat will go. Now we just need to decide when."

"Three days," I said. "That will give us time to beef up the armour on one of the vans and get the necessary supplies. I was going to take the cab, but I guess we're gonna need something bigger."

"I'll take care of that."

"Thank you, Roger," said Jules. "Is there anything else?"

There wasn't.

The meeting broke up, and the residents dispersed, talking quietly at the turn of events. Jules appeared at my side, grinning broadly.

"I told you, you would be surprised," he said.

"Smartass," I returned.

Three days flew past. We planned to go at daybreak on the fourth. On the last evening, we all gathered in the courtyard, and I finally got to have barbequed rabbit. I'd gone out twice and got lucky both times, thankfully without the canine interference. I bagged two rabbits by snares; the other three I shot.

"You okay?" Tina asked.

"I'm good," I said, chewing on a rabbit leg. "Despite being ganged up on."

She laughed. "All for a good cause. Do you think there will be any other refugees in Thamesmead?"

"It's a possibility, I guess. I've been looking for some sign of other groups every time I've gone out but nothing. I don't think everyone evacuated, especially in the more built-up areas. If there are other groups out there, it might be mutually advantageous to join forces. Firstly, for safety in numbers, but it would also bring more artisans into the mix and increase our chances of survival."

"Like you said, maybe we'll find them in Thamesmead. The land of more concrete, less grass."

"Exactly," I said. "I just wish we had some form of communication." I laughed bitterly. "I used to hate mobile phones and the internet; what I wouldn't give for thirty minutes worth right now."

"I know what you mean," said Tina. "I'm still checking my phone to see if I've got service!"

"I guess you really don't know what you've got until it's gone," I said ruefully, "but who knows what tomorrow will bring?"

"The eternal optimist. Just make sure you look after each other out there."

"It's going to be like a Sunday drive in the country," I assured her. "Thamesmead is less than an hour away under normal circumstances. We'll probably have to take a few detours, but I figure two hours at most."

"How long do you intend to stay there?"

"It'll probably be overnight. I want to check out the entire area. Hopefully we'll be able to find somewhere like the Block where we can maintain the community and keep everyone safe."

Kaminsky was across the courtyard slouching in a deck-chair outside of his flat, a beer in his fist. The rest of the six-pack lay under his seat. He was surreptitiously watching me and Tina, his expression not pleasant.

"You can stay at mine tonight if you want," Tina said, breaking into my thoughts. "No ties. Unless, of course, you want ties..." she added with a wicked grin.

The Block was buzzing with activity the following morning, people waiting to see us off. I had left Tina's very early so I could get my gear together. With my belt over one shoulder and the rifle over the other, Glock, Knife, and axe attached, I made my way to the van.

"Bloody hell!" quipped Charlie when he saw me. "You look like *The Last of the Mohicans*!"

I laughed. "If only this was North America! You make sure you've got a hat and sunglasses; the sun doesn't take prisoners."

"Will do, Kemosabe."

I didn't have the heart to tell Charlie that was *The Lone Ranger*. Nat appeared dressed in her usual Goth black, carrying a compound bow and a quiver of arrows.

"Nah, this ain't right!" Charlie was on a definite roll this morning. "First, we got *The Last of the Mohicans*, and now we've got a bloody ninja. If Kaminsky was coming with us, we'd have a full set!"

Everyone was laughing.

"Charlie! Behave!" Julie said, punching his shoulder playfully.

"You're laughing now, mate," retorted Nat, "but see if you're still laughing when a Creep's biting your arse and I'm all you've got!"

We stowed our gear in the van.

"I've put in a false floor," said Roger, "giving you space beneath for storage and a flat area on top for sleeping. There's memory foam mattresses for all of you, plus sleeping bags."

"Thanks, Roger. That's great," I said.

Food and water had already been loaded, and we were ready to roll when Jeff, carrying a long bundle wrapped in a blanket, motioned me to the rear of the van.

"I didn't want to openly hand these over," said Jeff, unwrapping the bundle. "Didn't want to send the wrong message. There's two shotguns; I'm afraid there's only ten shells between them. Then there's Smith and Wesson revolvers, thirty eights with three boxes of shells, two belts, and one shoulder rig."

"Wow," I said, looking at the guns, "hopefully we won't need them, but it's comforting to know we have a little firepower."

"There are more; Alan and I stashed them somewhere safe. We got them from a gun shop near Bexley. We cleaned it out. The shotguns came from the same farm as the chickens; that's why there's not a lot of ammo."

"You did right by keeping them to yourselves, but let Jules know about them."

"Will do," Jeff said. "Good luck."

I shook his hand. "We'll be a lot safer now. Thanks."

There were hugs all round before we got into the van, me driving. The last thing I saw as we drove through the arch was Kaminsky sitting on his motorbike, watching with his colourless eyes narrowed, the perpetual sneer on his mouth. I felt my nape hairs prickle.

It took all of twenty minutes to fuck up.

"We'll have to go around," I said, looking at the mass of vehicles deadlocked on the dual carriageway leading into Bexleyheath. "Head towards Mayplace Road and pick up Erith Road from there."

"Isn't that the long way round?" asked Nat.

"I was intending to go through Belvedere, but there's too much parkland. I thought this way would be better. I should have known it was a bad idea."

"Belvedere would have been the most direct route," said Charlie.

"It is," I sighed heavily, "and there's the problem. Everyone who knows the area headed that way. There's a roundabout notorious for accidents at the top end of the carriageway. I passed there a while back, and it was pretty jammed. I didn't want to risk going that way."

"We'll have to try going through Erith."

If it wasn't abandoned vehicles blocking the streets, it was vines sprouting from every garden and piece of waste ground, some straight up through the pavement. Slowly but surely, we were being forced farther and farther north.

"Adam," Nat said, indicating through the windscreen.

A pack of dogs were shadowing the van, eight or nine of the brutes, big mixed breeds. They looked to be starving as they kept pace with us, tongues lolling from slavering mouths, feral, half-crazed eyes bulging from ravaged faces.

"Fuck," breathed Charlie. "Are they the one's you saw?"

"No idea. These ones are bigger, and I saw only three."

"You said Thamesmead is bordered by the River Thames; why don't we get down to the water and find a boat?" suggested Nat.

"Because access to the river is severely limited," I said. "The nearest points are at Greenwich and Thamesmead itself. Besides, if we couldn't find a boat with an engine, we'd have to paddle upstream."

"Okay, Erith it is then," said Charlie.

I was never so glad to have air conditioning in a vehicle. I understated when I told Charlie the sun was merciless. There wasn't a word yet invented to describe the intense heat that shimmered off the concrete and turned the tarmac on the roads to taffy. The only benefit we had was that the heat drove the dog pack to cover, and we left them far behind.

After a lot of zigzagging and following a circuitous route back on the road to Erith, it was past mid-day when we finally got back on track

"Why are we stopping?" asked Charlie as I pulled over on top of a small flyover.

"I just want to check the area," I said, picking up the binoculars. "We're pretty safe up here; nothing can approach without our seeing it."

The road ahead was clear for about another two miles. Beyond that, I couldn't see. Panning the skyline, I couldn't see any other signs of life.

"Here," said Charlie, handing me a bottle of water. "Shit, this is creepy stuff," he said, peering over the flyover's protective wall.

South Erith spread out below us towards the west. Cars, vans, and various other vehicles were parked or abandoned haphazardly along the rubbish cluttered roads. The buildings were dark and forbidding, houses, shops, and municipal buildings with doors standing open and only shadows within. I could see vines encroaching through the streets, purple-black, insidious, creeping, weaving a deadly, impenetrable web; white thorns glittered in the bright sunlight, ever spreading.

"Oh man, look down there," said Charlie, pointing.

Nat and I both looked.

"Creeps," I muttered.

Three hundred yards away, the parkland below sprawled. It looked like school playing fields choked with dark shrubbery, oversized bushes bursting the boundaries of the school's perimeter, enveloping the buildings on every side. With them came the Creeps; dozens of them leaping from branch to branch, visible through breaks in the trees' canopy.

"Holy fuck," swore Charlie. "Where the hell are they all coming from? What are they after?"

"Us," said Nat, "and every living thing they can get their claws into."

"Now there's a charming thought," said Charlie.

I went to the rear of the van.

"Here, put these on." I held out two of the holstered revolvers.

Charlie's eyes popped open. "Jesus, Adam, what do I know about guns?"

"You point it, pull the trigger, and it goes bang. Hopefully, you'll hit what you're aiming at. What else do you need to know?"

Nat didn't have Charlie's reluctance as she avidly buckled on the holster.

"My dad was a soldier," she said. "I used to do a bit of target shooting with him."

"That explains the whole ninja thing then," quipped Charlie, shifting the gun belt to a more comfortable position around his lean waist. "I feel like Wyatt Earp."

Reaching the Erith Fish roundabout, I pulled over in the centre in the shadow of a huge, twenty-foot-high statue, depicting two intertwined bright blue mosaic fish.

"What are you thinking?" asked Nat.

"Bexley Road," I said, indicating the road straight across. "Bronze Age Way to the left and Walnut Tree Road situated between them; they all lead to Thamesmead."

"And?" asked Charlie.

"Frank's Park lies close to Bronze Age Way, and at the bottom of Bexley Road, there's Riverside Gardens, heavy greenery. I can't remember what's down Walnut Tree, except it joins West Street, which is also near Riverside Gardens. I'm not sure if it clears the parkland."

"You think the first two are likely to be overgrown?" asked Nat.

"A distinct possibility," I said.

"Then let's take the path of least resistance—take our chances with Walnut Tree Road. You never know. We might get lucky."

"Yeah, right," laughed Charlie.

It didn't help.

All three roads were dual carriageways with Walnut Tree Road being the smallest. Farther to the right was a row of warehouses beyond them the River Thames. Signs of severe scorching dotted the area; tiny islands of charred earth ran both sides of the carriageway and all along the

Town Hall. Trees stood stark, skeletal fingers reaching for the clear sky, blackened trunks cracked and split.

"Who do you think's responsible for that?" Charlie asked.

"God knows," answered Nat. "Look at this place. There's rubbish everywhere; it won't only be the vines choking the streets before long."

The van was loud in the preternatural silence as I drove on. Approaching the bottom, I slowed.

"Damn."

Riverside Gardens loomed ahead, alive with vines encroaching across the road. West Street was to the left.

"Just put your foot down and go," said Charlie. "There's room on the left-hand side of the road."

He was right. There was room, but I got the feeling we were burning our bridges. We might be able to pass now, but in a few days' time, I wasn't sure. The vines writhed and crunched under the tyres as we roared past into West Street.

"Jesus..." I slowed.

We were in a residential area; the road narrowed, terraced houses either side of us.

"Can you smell that?" I asked.

"Burning," said Charlie, powering down the window a little.

"Recent burning," said Nat. "You don't think the town's on fire, do you?"

"No," I said. "I can smell petrol as well, Molotov cocktails maybe, or possibly flamethrowers."

The eighteen-wheeler was jammed on a corner never meant to accommodate such a large vehicle. The white tractor bore a colourful mural of a mermaid smiling benignly at the world.

"Why the fuck would you bring a truck that big down these piddly side roads?" complained Charlie.

"It looks as if it's carrying tyres," said Nat.

"Yeah, I think there's a Kwik-Fit tyre centre round the back somewhere," I said.

"Great place to break down," said Charlie.

Mounting the kerb, I steered between the tractor and the Chinese Take-Away. A small junction was up ahead; a church with its steeple missing was on its farther side.

"Shit," I said. "I don't like the look of that."

The road forked, trees crowding in both directions, turning the road into a shadowy tunnel; the murk beneath was impenetrable.

"Looks quiet enough," said Charlie.

"I can't see anything moving," I said, using the binoculars, "but it's impossible to tell how long it stretches. Maybe we should turn back, find another route."

"Bollocks to that!" said Charlie. "It's taken nearly seven hours to get this far, a trip that should have taken less than an hour at most. How many more stops or diversions are we going to make? Do you know what's at the other end of the road?"

"If memory serves, there's a couple more roundabouts. We go right at the second, and it takes us straight to Church Manorway. From there, the industrial area's to the east towards the river," I said.

"Much green?" asked Nat.

"I can't be sure," I said. "It's already been a lot greener than I thought it would be."

"The black dust?" asked Charlie.

"Could well be," I said. "Which begs the question: How bad will it be beyond those trees?"

"Well, we can't sit here all day. I say we take our chances and drive through. If we don't stop or hang around, we should be okay," Charlie said.

I looked at Nat.

"You wanted to check out the entire area," she said. "We might as well start now."

Twenty-Two

Last day of November 2018

The vine lashed across the windscreen with a loud crack, vibrating the wire mesh with the impact, but the glass held.

"Fuck!"

Hauling on the steering wheel, I veered left as another vine whipped towards us. It missed the side window and drummed along the length of the van, making Nat and Charlie duck. We had barely gone a hundred yards beneath the trees when the onslaught started. Caught within the confines of the tunnel, there was no room to manoeuvre as the hideous undergrowth burst into life.

"Adam!" screamed Nat as a pile of rubble appeared in front of us, the remains of the church steeple. I caught a fleeting glimpse of the cross leaning drunkenly in a clump of writhing bushes.

Swerving around the debris, the rear of the van fish-tailed, bouncing on the loose bricks. Something rebounded off the side of the van; it sounded as if we were inside a drum. A quick look in the side mirror revealed a large Creep clinging to the van's roof.

"Look out!" yelled Charlie.

There was only a brief moment to register the dark shape hurtling towards the windscreen. Clawed fingers gripped the wire mesh, and an insane face glared through

the glass in a silent roar, wicked teeth dripping venomous saliva in thick stringy ropes. The mesh rattled as the Creep threw itself violently side to side in a maniacal attempt to tear the metal off the front of the speeding van. Charlie levelled his revolver at the brute.

"No!" I yelled. "The windshield!"

Pulling on the windscreen wiper, two jets of water spurted from the bonnet nozzles and surprised the Creep into releasing its grip. Heaving to the left, the creature rolled off and tumbled onto the unforgiving road. A quarter of a mile farther on, the trees thinned. The road was blocked by two cars; a Ford Sierra was buried into the side of another vehicle. Dark shapes flew through the branches on either side of us, easily keeping pace. A loud buckling of metal signalled a second Creep had landed on the roof; another struck the side.

"Hold on!" I yelled, aiming for the widest gap between the crashed cars and the metal railings lining the pavement.

A wild cacophony filled the interior of the van as Creeps pounded relentlessly on the roof and side panels. There was a violent jolt as I clipped the rear of the Sierra, spinning it away as I fought to maintain control. It catapulted a Creep through the air, dislodging it off the roof by the impact. A fierce surge of joy tore through me as I saw the flailing body smash into a lamp post; dark blood flew.

Tyres squealing, I righted the van, stamping down on the accelerator. Nearing the end of the trees, two concrete barriers appeared, angling into the road and leaving a wide gap in the centre. Rocketing forward, I ducked involuntarily as twin sheets of flame seared past the van into the trees, saturating them with liquid fire.

"Jesus!" yelled Charlie, throwing himself over Nat protectively.

The back end of the van swung around as I braked hard, bringing it to a dead stop. Two soldiers with flamethrowers were standing behind the concrete barriers dousing the trees in short, savage bursts as another squad rained automatic fire into the foliage. Several charred bodies dropped out of the branches, lost in the glare of the flames and smoke covering the ground.

Stepping out of the van, the gunfire was deafening; the heat of the flamethrowers caught in my throat. Then everything fell quiet; there was only the crackling of burning wood and the stink of seared flesh. Charlie and Nat joined me whilst the soldiers continued to cover the roadway and trees.

"Jesus H. Christ..." murmured Charlie.

"Don't move!" The voice was commanding, authoritative.

We turned as an army captain, flanked by two armed soldiers, stepped out of a jeep. Three armoured vehicles pulled up behind him.

"What the devil are you doing here? This is a restricted area. Who are you?" he demanded.

More soldiers piled out of one of the armoured vehicles and took up positions behind the officer. Automatic weapons were raised.

"Whoa there, Sunshine!" Charlie said, raising his hands. "We're on your side."

"Sergeant!" barked the captain.

The sergeant came forward and relieved us of our guns.

"Aw man," said Charlie, "I was just getting used to wearing that!"

Ignoring Charlie, the soldier returned to the ranks.

"We're civilians, looking for somewhere safe to settle," I said.

"Settle?" asked the officer.

"Live," I said.

"Where have you come from?"

"Just this side of Wellingham, New Leaf Sheltered Housing. The name's Blake, Adam Blake. This is Charlie Donovan and Natalie Morrison."

"Nat," she corrected.

"I'm Captain James Williams, Special Recon and Expedition Force. Why aren't you in one of the enclaves?"

"What enclaves?" I asked.

"The Isle of Dogs, City of London, and Hyde Park; all refugees have been directed to those three camps, where you should be."

"Been there, done that, didn't like it," said Charlie.

"Been where exactly?" asked Williams.

"Queen Elizabeth's Hospital," Charlie answered. "It was a shambles."

"Queen Elizabeth's has been closed down for eight and a half months," said Williams.

"I'm not surprised," Charlie said. Turning to me, he said, "At least the rumours were right. Utilizing the City, I wonder if the other rumours panned out."

"We can't stay here," Williams said. "We're bivouacked a mile and a half away. You…" he pointed at Charlie, "you'll ride in the A.T.V.; my sergeant will go with your friends."

"Now hold up…" Charlie began.

"Charlie, it's okay. Just do as he says; we'll sort it later," I said.

Charlie nodded and was escorted to one of the All-Terrain Vehicles. Nat and I got back in the van with the sergeant. He was a big, grim-faced man with hard eyes. We dropped into line as the vehicles pulled out just as evening was beginning to fall.

They were camped between two long warehouses on one of the many industrial estates along Bronze Age Way. The leading vehicles peeled away, disappearing behind one of the buildings.

"Park over there," ordered the sergeant whose name tag identified him as "Strickland."

The area was fortified at both ends; the two lines of warehouses on either side afforded ready protection. Three large army trucks blocked the farther end, while heavy wooden trestles bristling with razor wire barred access from the side we entered, the trestles being moved manually as needed. Four machine gun nests occupied positions on the roof of the warehouses, covering all angles. Armed sentries paced the perimeter, and six freestanding search-lights illuminated the whole scene as evening began to fall.

Williams approached with Charlie in tow. He led us to one of the brightly lit units that had been commandeered as a base of operations. A quick glance showed that the three other units were being used as a canteen, mess hall, and a barracks.

"Please, be seated," Williams said.

"Is there a problem?" I asked.

"That's what I need to ascertain," the soldier said, throwing his bright red beret onto the makeshift desk and rubbing the back of his head.

Two soldiers followed us into the unit, placing our guns on a long camp table against one wall. They had the shotguns and Nat's bow and arrows.

"I'm surprised to still find people out here," Williams said, settling into a camp chair. "Most people have already been evacuated, which prompts the question: Why weren't you?"

"I told you, we tried that. It wasn't for us," said Charlie.

"You said. So, what are your intentions?"

"Relocate to a safe area," I said.

"There isn't one outside of the enclaves," Williams said emphatically. "Which prompts a second question: Why would you want to stay out here?"

"If you've got something to say, then say it," I said. "Stop beating around the bush; you've obviously got something on your mind, so ask."

Williams steepled his fingers under his chin and regarded me probingly.

"Some of our supply runs have been attacked, looted. It's more a nuisance than a problem."

"You think we're looters?" cut in Charlie.

"Frankly, no. I was hoping you could shed some light on the attacks," Williams said.

"They're stealing guns?" asked Nat.

"No, ordinance is shipped under heavy armed guard. It's mainly field equipment, tents, uniforms, mess kits, that sort of thing," said Williams.

"They're random attacks then?" I asked.

"Random, uncoordinated, targeting one and two truck runs. As I said, more of a nuisance," Williams said.

"Sorry, mate. It's not us," Charlie said.

"What happens now? Why are you holding us?" asked Nat.

"I'm not," said Williams. "Just following procedure. This area has been designated a red zone."

"What does that mean?" I asked.

"Uninhabitable," Williams said, standing up. "You've already encountered part of the reason. Let me show you the rest."

He flipped a concealing sheet of paper over the free-standing whiteboard behind him.

"London," he said, indicating the map pinned to the board.

"That's a lot of red," said Charlie.

The city was almost surrounded by a solid circle of red, southwest towards Surrey especially. The southeast was patchy until it passed the M25 Orbital where it became more prevalent. The north was very patchy with a solid line cutting through the bright colour running parallel with the M1 and A1 motorways.

"We are continually torching the Northern Passage, maintaining access to and from the city, but we are fighting a losing battle," said Williams. "As you can see, Central and West London are clear. To achieve this, we basically destroyed Hyde Park. The Isle of Dogs is also clear and so is some of east London, except around Victoria Park and moving farther north, Epping Forest." He pointed to an area in the southeast sector of the city. "Greenwich, Blackheath, Plumstead, and here..." he tapped with his finger, "Thamesmead."

The north, west and southwest of the borough were red.

"The map hasn't been updated today," Williams said. "You can now include the south and southeast."

"Shit," Charlie said quietly.

"That's not good," echoed Nat.

"I strongly advise you to rethink your plans of relocation," Williams said, sitting down. "Go to one of the enclaves. Be safe."

"And grossly overcrowded," said Charlie.

"Hyde Park, Central London, and the Isle of dogs," I said. "How the hell have you managed to make room for all the people in just three locations? It's not possible."

A brief, shocked expression crossed Williams' face as he glanced quickly at his sergeant standing by the door and then back to me.

"Mr. Blake..." he began.

"Adam."

"Adam," he said, clearing his throat. "Are you not aware of the casualties?"

"Casualties? What are you talking about?"

Before he even spoke, a coldness enveloped my body; I barely suppressed a shudder.

"After the initial deluge of black dust, there was a relative period of quiet. Then the storm hit. Then the vines. Then the Creeps appeared."

"We know all that," Nat cut him short. "Get to the point."

Williams looked uncomfortable. "What you might not know is that the rural areas of England were hit days before the Dust reached the bigger cities. Towns, villages, all of them were completely overrun before we were even aware of what was happening.

"The cities were next." He stopped, seeing the horrified impatience on our faces.

"Eighty percent of the U.K.'s population was lost in the first nine weeks after the deluge and storm, mostly due to the vines, partly because of the Creeps."

The shocked silence was complete. I was heard the words, but the magnitude of their meaning wouldn't register; my throat locked, and I was numb.

"That's not possible," Nat said in a breathless whisper.

"I'm afraid it is," Williams said. "Because of the lack of communication, people were totally unaware of the danger. Thousands of lives were lost. Hundreds of small, rural towns were wiped out; lines of access, roads, trains, and waterways were cut. By the time we mobilised, it was already too late; we were caught like rats in a trap."

"Was it just the U.K. or were other places affected, other countries?" I stammered.

"We don't know for certain. England, Cornwall, and the Midlands for sure. As for the rest, we can only assume. As far as I know, there has been no contact whatsoever with the outside world."

My worst fears were dragged screaming and kicking into the light. I had ignored what my gut was telling me since the beginning. I was living in false hope, the only thing left to me, and that had just been brutally torn away. Looking at each other, I wondered if I was as pale as Nat and Charlie and if they were as numb as I was.

"We need to get back," Charlie said. "Julie, the kids…"

"I wouldn't advise that," said Williams. "It's getting dark; you'll never make it."

"Fuck the dark!" Charlie shouted abruptly, getting to his feet, his chair clattered to the floor behind him. "My family's back there!"

"Charlie, he's right," I said sharply. "It's too dangerous. It won't do them any good if we're dead. We'll go at first light."

"Adam…"

"First light," I said.

"Your friend is a little hot-headed," Williams said as we sat in the mess.

"He's a family man," I said, nursing my coffee. "Believe me, I'm just as anxious to get back to the Block as he is."

"I can understand that; I lost my family to the dust."

"I'm sorry," I said.

"You know what the scary thing is? I've no idea what this is all about, how it started, who the hell the enemy is. The dust, the vines, those … Creeps."

"I guess we'll never know," I said, "but knowing is no longer the point; dealing with it is."

"Dealing with it? Is that what you think we're doing?" Williams scoffed. "Come with me."

Leaving Charlie and Nat sleeping in one of the other units, I followed Williams out of the mess into a shadowy unit filled with electronic equipment across the way.

"Everything is logged and recorded," he explained as we passed two soldiers manning various glowing monitors, both wearing earphones. "Under normal circumstances, you wouldn't even know this data existed, let alone view it, but I think you need to see it. It'll help you decide your next course of action."

Sitting at an unmanned station, Williams clicked on an icon on the computer's desktop, one of dozens of video files.

"This was taken yesterday," he said.

Nothing could have prepared me for that video.

"Bravo Two, no contact, proceeding to sector four."

The footage was jerky, black and white. Soldiers were moving ahead between several large warehouses, but they were different from the one we were in. Two lines, keeping close to the sheltering walls, the soldiers heavily armed. The leader paused at the corner and held a fist upright.

"Contact! Contact!"

The area opened into a broad concrete car park. On the farther side by the river, a huge mass of vines unlike any I had seen so far writhed and twisted, massive fronds lashing the air. They were huge, as thick as a man's thigh, rearing twenty, maybe twenty-five feet into the air. They enveloped the entire riverbank as far as the eye could see. They sprawled over the buildings; metal screeched, roof panels crumpled, concrete collapsed. The slithering plants stretched hundreds of yards, wrapping thorn-encrusted fronds over walls, around lampposts, through storage sheds, and crushing them all with ease.

"Jesus," I breathed.

"Incoming!" barked the communication speaker.

Three soldiers knelt, weapons raised, firing in short static bursts. The rest of the soldiers took up positions, the chatter of their automatic rifles joining the barrage, firing at the unseen enemy.

One of the soldiers screamed and staggered backwards with what appeared to be a spear lodged in his chest. Gunfire crackled through the computer's speakers; the picture became erratic.

"Flamers! Get the fucking flamers up here!"

The mouth of the alley was alive with swift moving figures, bright flashes of gunfire, screams, and curses. The soldier wearing the body cam flew backwards, there was a grunt, and the picture was still.

Several soldiers were down as others made an orderly retreat. A monstrous shape filled the screen, silently roaring, glaring red and black eyes, a gaping, foaming mouth. In its furred, clawed hand, it gripped a long, white stick, slick with venom, needle sharp.

The screen went black.

"They're using thorns as spears," I said incredulously.

"With devastating effect," Williams said. "We kill them in droves, but they just keep coming. They're reckless, fearless, and totally unheeding of our weapons. Did you notice anything else?"

I thought for a second as the horrific scenes played through my mind.

"They broke cover," said Williams. "It's happened several times during recent confrontations. They can't do it for long and only in the sun's dying rays. They're getting bolder, bigger; they're adapting."

"The vines are massive," I said.

"And getting bigger, more voracious. Other discoveries have been made. The Creeps do communicate with one another on a higher frequency beyond human hearing, a little like a dog whistle was how it was explained to me at a recent briefing. The size of the vines is believed to be connected to the storm after the initial deluge."

"How?" I asked.

"The Dust settled on every surface, some of which were incapable of absorbing it: stone, concrete, etcetera. When the storm came, it was all washed into the sewers..."

"Which drain into the Thames," I finished.

"Tons of it, concentrated into a narrow strip of flowing water."

"Maybe that explains why all the domestic amenities were shut down except the water; was it because they needed it?" I wondered.

"I lost nine men in that attack yesterday. We killed dozens of Creeps; the flamers are our best defence. There's a symbiotic link between the vines and the Creeps. They work together, protecting each other, advancing, growing, and gaining more and more ground while we are being slowly pushed back. The brutes are immune to the venom on the thorns; for us, the slightest scratch is fatal. We discovered the Creeps do not like the cold, hence this damned heat. One was captured in North London after it got clipped in the head by a stray bullet. They caged it and took it for examination. It woke up in transit and went into a berserk rage, and it didn't stop until it bashed its own brains out on the bars of the cage. The damned things are insane."

"Have any plans been made to stop them?" I asked.

Williams rubbed wearily at his face. "I need some coffee," he said.

The night air was humid. Sweat irritated the back of my neck beneath my ponytail. The mess was empty except for two soldiers at the far table. They watched as we got some coffee.

"The situation is desperate," Williams said once we were seated. "Which is why I can't emphasise enough that you should get your people to an enclave as soon as possible. What you've seen here is just the tip of the iceberg. Other areas, the New Forest and Epping Forest, for instance, are totally lost. All forest and woodland areas are irrecoverable, impenetrable. Gas, chemicals, none of it works. There's only one infallible solution against the vines and the Creeps ... fire."

"You can't be serious?" I said. "The end result would be catastrophic. The loss of so many trees. How would it even be possible?"

"Plans have been proposed, though nothing has been finalised, which is why teams like mine are out on fact-finding expeditions."

"What about the people? Are you suggesting that they're to be sacrificed?"

"Good God, no," Williams said. "There will be a mass evacuation of all civilians by sea, cruise ships, tankers, the Navy. Every vessel possible is to be commandeered to get the people out safely."

"That's crazy. It's not possible."

"I obviously haven't all the details, but it will happen. Project Inferno is our only hope."

"And what's Project Inferno?" I asked, not really wanting to know the answer.

"An aerial bombardment of the densest areas of vine infestation utilizing thermobaric devices," said Williams.

"Firebombs?" I asked.

"In layman's terms, yes, but these devices are exponentially more efficient."

He sounded proud of the horrific weapon they were proposing to unleash on an unsuspecting city.

"When's this operation going to commence, and which areas are targeted?"

"I've been given six days to pull my troops out of this area, the south and southwest," said Williams. "Which is why you need to evacuate immediately."

"Six days? What about the refugee camps? Won't they be in the drop zone?"

"The camps are perfectly safe and well outside the strike areas. They'll be evacuated long before phase two commences."

"Can you hear what you are saying? This is insane," I said. "You're endangering the entire city. You'll never be able to contain the aftermath of such a bombardment; the whole of London will burn."

"Mr. Blake, I think those in authority are fully aware of every aspect of this operation and have taken any and all precautions into consideration. They are in possession of all the necessary data, which will be complete once I return to Central Command. I assure you, you needn't worry. Soon everything will be returning to normal. The vines, along with the Creeps, will be destroyed, and we will have London back."

I was at a loss for words. I stared into his calm, assured face as the chill slowly enveloped my entire body, tickling my nape hairs, making me shudder. The realization slowly seeped into my brain.

He believes. He truly believes... God help us all.

Twenty-Three

December 1st 2018

Sleep was impossible. I paced the unit in stocking feet not wishing to wake Nat and Charlie. My mind was awhirl. Surely, Williams must see the failings in the so-called evacuation plan; it was nonsense. The shocking revelation that so many had already died rocked me, but even so, there still must be hundreds, if not thousands, of refugees still in the camps. How were they supposed to meet the ships and boats allegedly being sent to evacuate them off mainland England? The Thames was already choked with giant vines, and Creeps roamed freely through the city; there was no clear path. It wasn't just crazy—it was suicide.

The time before dawn was hot, uncomfortably humid. Within seconds of wiping the clinging sweat from my face and neck, I was wet again. Williams had returned our weapons, and having the Glock on my hip was becoming more and more reassuring. Like the profanity, it was a familiar friend. Sitting in a camp chair by the unit entrance, I watched the activity across the way in the mess room. Cooks were preparing breakfast, firing up field stoves, boiling water for tea and coffee; I could smell it from here.

"Hey." Charlie rubbed his thinning hair as he sat up on his bunk.

"Good morning," I greeted. "Sleep well?"

"Fuck did I," he said, swinging his legs round and fumbling for his boots. "It's like trying to sleep on a narrow plank."

"You seemed to be managing all right." I grinned.

"I try not to complain," he said. "I could do with a cuppa."

"They're just sorting breakfast now," I said.

"Didn't you sleep?" he asked, pulling up a chair.

"We've got a problem," I said.

"That makes a change," Charlie said.

"I'm serious, Charlie. I was up most of the night talking to Captain Williams. He showed me some video footage, and it's bad."

"What's going on?" he asked, seeing the worry in my face.

"Wake up, Nat. You both need to hear this."

We sat in a huddle, Nat still rubbing the sleep out of her eyes. I had gotten some tea for us in white Styrofoam cups, and it helped wake her up while I told them about the previous night's events.

"Williams is in denial," I said. "Either that or he is blindly accepting that his superiors know what they're doing. I'm not a hundred percent sure he is in control of his faculties. There's massive holes in this evacuation plan, but he's just not seeing it, or he doesn't want to."

"The giant vines aren't just local?" Nat asked.

"No, I saw footage of Greenwich, and it's a jungle. There's no way past it, same along both sides of the Thames. The river is completely blocked. I doubt if a small boat could pass, let alone ships and cruise liners. I haven't seen it, but I'm guessing Tower Bridge isn't up."

"So nothing big can get past it," said Charlie.

"Maybe they're going to be airlifted out," suggested Nat.

"If there's anything still flying," I said. "Helicopters would be the best bet, but it could take days, if not weeks, to get everybody out; it doesn't seem feasible to me."

"Something's not right. Why hasn't an evacuation already started? It's been ten months."

"It doesn't look good for the Block," Nat said. "If the vines are that big, soon even fire won't be a deterrent."

"We need to get back," said Charlie. "Put our heads together. Figure this thing out."

The camp was coming alive as light grew. Going over to the mess unit, we had a quick breakfast, eager to be off.

The general atmosphere was one of efficient familiarity; the men went about their duties like clockwork, months of continual expeditions making every day's duties second nature. They ate in small groups, quietly talking and keeping their weapons incongruously close at hand while seeming unperturbed by the present situation.

Williams appeared, groomed, clean shaven, his uniform immaculate; it somehow looked and felt wrong. He saw us in the mess, and with a quick smile, he headed our way.

The machine gun fire stopped him mid-stride and startled the hell out of me.

"Incoming!" bellowed one of the machine gun nests on the roof.

Harsh, stuttering gunfire ripped the air. The response was immediate; the soldiers grabbed their weapons and rushed to their assigned positions.

"Flamers! South perimeter!" Williams's voice was loud over the gunfire. "Move yourselves!"

Small arms fire joined the cacophony. Men yelled and took cover as a shower of white spears clattered on the concrete between the warehouses, bouncing off vehicles with loud clangs.

"Watch out for the venom!" I shouted at Charlie, who was crouching by the unit's door. A spear rattled on the ground close by. Nat knelt beside me.

A line of soldiers knelt by the razor wire, firing sporadic bursts. I saw fleeting glimpses of Creeps milling about beyond the defences, hurling white thorns and ducking out of sight. A soldier screamed, falling backwards, his weapon dropping to the ground as he clutched at the spear buried in his right shoulder. The gunfire intensified, the noise deafening.

"Over there!" Charlie was pointing towards the trucks at the other end of the camp. I could see figures beneath the vehicles, stealthily stalking the unsuspecting soldiers from behind.

Holding the Glock with two hands, I opened fire. I think I hit two of the brutes, but in the confusion I couldn't be sure. Discovered, the Creeps rushed from cover. Charlie moved to the cover of a pile of crates stacked outside the unit, firing randomly as he went. Nat slipped across to take the place he had vacated. The machine gun on the roof above us saw the new danger and redirected their fire; Creeps dropped like sacks of potatoes.

Ducking down behind the crates, Charlie fumbled to reload. In that second, he was blind to the Creep charging towards his position.

"Charlie!" I yelled, but I was too late.

The Creep cleared the crates and knocked Charlie off his feet with a slashing claw. He rolled, coming to his knees, his gun flying from his hands. I took aim but had no shot; Charlie was kneeling between me and the Creep!

The white thorn glittered in the creature's hand as it raised the spear high above its bullethead for the killing blow. Aghast, Charlie watched helplessly.

"Charlie!" I yelled again, my heart leaping into my throat.

The arrow appeared in the brute's chest as if by magic, struck through the heart, quivering. The Creep staggered back, its awful eyes wide with shock as it crashed into the pile of crates, its gnarled fingers clutching feebly at the shaft as it sank lifelessly to the ground.

Nat was there, offering Charlie a helping hand up, a big grin on her face.

"Told ya!" She winked as they got to cover.

Charlie's face was the colour of sour cream as he crouched by the wall of the unit. He was shaking so badly that he had to put his gun on the ground.

The gunfire slackened and then stopped.

"You okay?" I asked, kneeling next to Charlie.

"Jesus..." he croaked, "that was close. I thought I was a goner for sure."

"Never," I said. "Not while we've got a ninja."

Charlie's smile was sickly.

"We're here for each other," Nat said, putting a comforting arm on his shoulder.

"Everyone okay?" Williams appeared behind us.

"Just about," I said, rising. "What the hell was that?"

"I don't know," said Williams. "First time we've actually experienced a daylight attack. I told you, they're getting bolder."

"We need to leave," I said.

"As do I," said Williams. "Walk with me."

We headed for the van as soldiers wearing thick rubber gloves gingerly moved the venomous thorns littering the ground out of harm's way. There were three casualties, all fatal. A dozen Creeps lay in pools of their own blood. Soldiers were breaking camp, loading equipment onto the lorries, stowing supplies.

"I wish I could offer you an escort back," Williams said, "but it's imperative I get all the collected data back to Central Command. What I can do is offer you some supplies: food, ordinance, radios."

"Radios?" I echoed.

"Yes. Six handsets and a transmitter, plus half a dozen automatic weapons and ammunition. It's the best I can do. Once again, I strongly advise you take your people to the nearest enclave. I received orders this morning that I am to return immediately. Operation Inferno has been given the go-ahead; I'm to help supervise the evacuation."

I wanted to tell him that I thought the evacuation was never going to happen and that Operation Inferno was a terrible mistake, but seeing the absolute belief on his face, I didn't voice my thoughts. At the van, I saw the rear doors were open and several boxes and crates had been placed inside. Williams opened one of the crates and produced an automatic rifle.

"Have you any experience with one of these?" he asked.

I shook my head.

"They're simple enough," he said. "Magazine here, till it clicks, pull here, gun ready. Safety, automatic fire, semi-automatic. Got it?"

I watched as he took me through it again.

"Don't fire in long bursts; short, three second bursts are better." Williams put the gun back in the box. "The radios are self-explanatory. You shouldn't have any trouble with them. The range is about a mile radius, and batteries are rechargeable."

"We can't thank you enough," I said, shaking his hand.

"Just get to an enclave. Be safe," he said, nodding at Charlie and Nat he walked off and resumed barking orders.

"Do you think the Creeps are still about?" asked Nat as we pulled out.

"We'll just have to keep our eyes open. Keep moving," I said.

I felt a little twinge as I saw the army trucks roll out behind us. They went north; we headed south. I suddenly felt vulnerable, but then I thought of our friends back at the Block.

"What are we going to do now that Thamesmead is a washout?" asked Charlie. "Stay at the Block?"

"Staying there is not an option, Charlie. Nothing's changed except we have to rethink where we can go," I said.

"It's not a total loss," said Nat. "At least we have radios, weapons. We're better off now than when we started out."

I smiled inwardly, glad of her optimism.

"Well, that sucks," said Charlie, looking at the fallen lamppost across the road, blocking our path.

"That wasn't there earlier," said Nat.

"No, it wasn't," I said, wondering the implications of it. "We'll have to backtrack."

We had already passed the place where we had met Williams and his men and dropped down to rejoin Bronze Age Way farther on. Erith lay ahead. There was so much debris, it was dangerous to go faster than thirty miles an hour, even though I was anxious to get back.

We weaved through a series of backstreets and had to detour twice due to obstructions, mainly abandoned cars, before finally coming out onto Bexley Road. The greenery around us was sporadic. There was evidence of burning, but it was haphazard; the job had not been thorough.

Nat was sitting by the passenger window and looking intently at the passing landscape, continually looking back.

"Nat?" I queried.

"I think we're being followed," she said.

Immediately glancing into the side and rearview mirrors, I looked for movement on the road behind us.

"I don't see anything," I said.

"Not on the road," she said. "It's on the other side of the trees, pacing us."

"Creeps?" asked Charlie, peering through the windscreen.

"I don't know. I can't get a good look at them, just a blur, but they're moving fast."

"Keep an eye out. We'll be at the Erith Fish Roundabout soon; the going will be easier after that."

The road dipped, cutting through a low hill; ornamental concrete cladding rose either side of us, obscuring our view of the surrounding area. My peripheral vision caught the sun reflecting off glass, and I braked hard, causing the van to lurch to a stop before I realised why. A dark green saloon car bounced down the incline as we exited the underpass. It barrelled onto the road ahead and was immediately followed by a shower of spears dropping out of the sky.

"Christ! There's dozens of the fuckers!" yelled Charlie as dark shapes piled over the top of the embankment.

"Hold on!"

Gunning the engine, I floored the accelerator and veered right, heading straight for a gap in the central meridian. Bodies struck the van and fists pounded on the sides before being thrown off as I fought the steering wheel. We careened over the rough ground beyond the roadway, cutting across to a small side road. The tyres squealed as they made contact with the road. Bringing the van around, I stamped on the gas again, rocketing away from the immediate danger.

"Did you see that?" bawled Charlie. "Did you see that? The bastards ambushed us! They fucking ambushed us. That's mad! Holy fucking shit!"

"They're still coming," said Nat. "They're taking to the trees."

"We've got to get off this road," I said, seeing more trees ahead of us. "Find a place to hide for a while, get them off our backs."

Various industrial estates lay on our right side. I hauled right into an access road, immediately turned right past two units, then turned left, and then right again.

"There!" exclaimed Charlie, pointing to an open warehouse.

Passing the entrance, I shoved the van into reverse and backed into the unit. Nat and Charlie leapt out and swiftly closed the warehouse shutters. Turning off the engine, we waited, holding our breath tensely to see if we would be discovered.

"This is crazy," whispered Charlie as we sat in the front of the van. "We're being hunted by educated space monkeys! How are they evolving so quickly?"

"I don't know," I said, leaning back in the driver's seat. "We're being surprised at every turn by something new."

"What if they learn about guns?" asked Nat. "There will be no stopping them."

"We can't stop them now," Charlie said bleakly.

Nat slipped out of the van and went to the warehouse door to peer out of section of cutaway panels that ran horizontally across the shutters and gave a view to the outside. She hastily backed away, her finger on her lips.

"There's a Creep on the roof of the warehouse opposite," she said. "It's just sitting there; I think it's on its own."

"They know we're here somewhere; they just don't know where," I said.

We waited. Sitting in the van as the day wore on, the temperature in the warehouse slowly rose. The heat became oppressive, and perspiration soaked our bodies uncomfortably. The unit wasn't large, about a hundred by fifty feet; metal benches were fixed to the left-hand wall, stud partitioning formed a small office at the rear, with a single toilet in the corner. The place was becoming an oven.

"We could shoot it," Charlie said, wiping his face for the umpteenth time with a white handkerchief already damp with sweat.

"Too far and too noisy," I said, peering at the creature.

"Nat's got her bow," Charlie said.

You had to admire his optimistic persistence.

"I'll shoot it through one of the holes in the door, shall I?" whispered Nat. "That'll work."

"We've got to do something," Charlie said. "We can't just sit here."

"Yes, we can," I said.

As the afternoon wore on, I was seriously considering Charlie's suggestion of shooting the damned thing. It just sat there, seemingly oblivious to the scorching sun and suffocating heat, not eating, not drinking, just watching.

"Doesn't it even want to pee?" complained Charlie. "Jesus!"

"It's a predator, a hunter; patience comes natural to it," I said.

"There's a side door," Nat said. "Maybe I should try with the bow."

I was tempted to agree.

"We don't know how many are out there," I said instead. "For all we know, they could be on every roof. It's too risky."

"Then let's make a run for it," said Charlie.

"I want to get out of here, Charlie, but it's impossible. As soon as we start to raise the shutters, that bastard will be alerted and raise the alarm; the doors are too solid to smash through.

We're just going to have to wait it out."

Nat shaking my shoulder brought me out of an uneasy sleep.

"It's gone," she said quietly.

I got out of the back of the van and crept to the shutters. The sun had just risen, the sky a pale blue. The rooftop opposite was empty. Charlie was moving along the shutter trying to get different views, but the line of sight was very limited.

"There's no sign of anything," he said.

"I can go out the side door, check that the coast is clear," Nat offered.

"No, I'll go," I said.

She shook her head. "You cover me; shoot only if absolutely necessary. I can use my bow if it's still lurking about."

I wasn't happy, but it made sense.

"Okay, Charlie, get ready to raise the shutters, but do it slowly, quietly."

The side door creaked as Nat eased it open, peering tentatively out, looking in all directions, especially up. Bow ready, she stepped out into the open, hugging the wall; I took up a position near the door. Backing down the alley between the buildings, Nat watched for any sign of movement, her bow following her eyes. I stepped out of the doorway, feeling the relief of a cool breeze on my face as Nat got to the centre of the alley. She stood, head cocked, listening; looking at me, she shook her head.

Giving Charlie the thumbs up, I went to the corner of the building. Nat and I covered each other as the shutter began to rise. My heart was beating like a hammer in my chest as I looked from rooftop to rooftop, expecting at any minute to see a horde of ravening monsters rushing towards me in a horrible silent charge, madness in their eyes.

The shutters were fully raised. I motioned for Nat and Charlie to get into the van. I quickly followed.

Twenty-Four

December 2018

It was nerve-wracking as we slowly drove out of the industrial estate, all eyes watching the rooftops. It took every bit of willpower I had not to gun the engine and go, but experience told me *softly, softly, catchee monkey*; in this case, I needed to put as much distance as possible between us and them, quietly.

"Thank Christ for that," said Charlie, chugging on a bottle of water. "I thought we were never going to get out of that place."

"Ugh!" grimaced Nat, a look of disgust on her face. "This water is so warm, I could make tea with it!"

Charlie laughed. It was a good sound, momentarily banishing the situation from our minds as we all laughed.

"I wish," said Charlie. "I could do with a cuppa!"

Home was in sight. Bexleyheath was three miles behind us after driving most of the day, stopping only once for a brief bite to eat. The atmosphere in the van was sombre, each of us thinking of the last two days, eager to be home, but not looking forward to breaking the news.

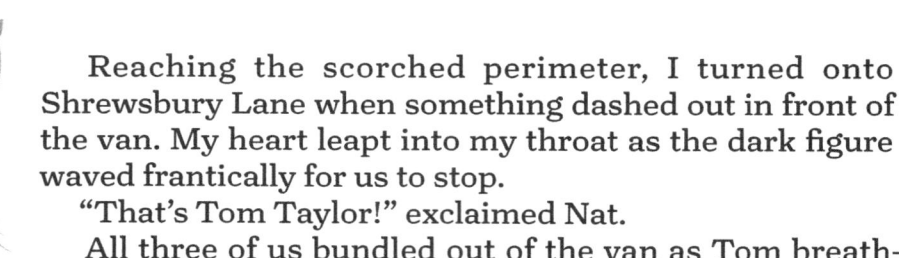

Reaching the scorched perimeter, I turned onto Shrewsbury Lane when something dashed out in front of the van. My heart leapt into my throat as the dark figure waved frantically for us to stop.

"That's Tom Taylor!" exclaimed Nat.

All three of us bundled out of the van as Tom breathlessly ran up to us.

"Adam! Thank God!" he gasped. "The Block, we've got trouble."

"Did I do something wrong in a previous life or something?" said Charlie. "This is never ending."

"Calm down, Charlie," I said. "Tell me again, Tom. You say there's nine of them now?"

"Yeah, I was right behind you as you left, or I would have been caught in the Block too. I needed some electrical supplies, so I was headed to a place on the outskirts of Eltham. I'd only gone about half a mile when I heard motorbike engines, lots of them. I circled back just in time to see Kaminsky greeting a bunch of bikers outside the Block, seven of them, rough looking bastards. They rode into the Block and closed the arch with the bus; it's been like that ever since."

"What made you stay outside?" asked Nat.

"The shouting," Tom said. "Seeing those bikers felt off right from the start, so I waited a bit, getting as close as I could without being seen. I heard shouting, voices raised in anger, then a woman's scream."

"Son of a bitch," said Charlie. "The screaming, did you recognise who it was?"

"No," said Tom, "there was too much noise."

"Were they armed?" I asked.

"I don't think so. A couple of them had crossbows slung on their backs, but I didn't see any guns," Tom said.

"Then we can go in with guns, throw 'em all out," said Charlie fiercely.

"You can't," said Tom, pulling a piece of crumpled paper out of his pocket and handing it to me. "I've spent the last two nights out here but kept watch every morning at first light. That first morning there was a commotion on the roof. My son Paul threw a thermos flask into the road. I saw where it fell. They dragged him off the roof. A few minutes later, a couple of the bikers came out and started searching for the flask, but they couldn't find it. I waited until evening and retrieved it. That letter was inside."

Charlie and Nat peered over my shoulder as I read the hastily written note aloud.

"Kaminsky has separated the women from the men, locked them up. He's holding all the children as hostages in Jules' flat so everyone cooperates. They're not armed, just knives, machetes, clubs, and two crossbows. They know Adam has a gun. They're waiting for him to come back. They are going to use the kids as leverage to make you surrender."

"Why would he do this?" asked Nat. "We were sharing, happy to give them shelter, food; there's no need for violence."

"For some people, it's the only way," I said. "I should have known. That's where all the missing food went; Kaminsky took it to feed his men on the outside, just waiting for us to leave."

"Let's give a show of force," said Charlie. "Show him he hasn't got a chance."

"We can't let Kaminsky know we have guns, especially automatics," I said. "He stands on the roof with a knife at one of the kid's throats, what are we gonna do?"

"Our own security has stymied us," said Tom. "We did too good a job; we can't get past it."

"Well, that's not strictly true," I said.

They all looked at me, and I grinned.

It seemed like all I was doing lately was waiting impatiently for time to pass. Evening was a long time coming. Retreating back to a house that Tom had been using as a refuge a couple of streets away, we sat about the grate, staring at the ashes of a long dead fire. Blankets had been nailed over the windows, so our flashlights wouldn't be seen from the outside.

Making coffee with the supplies given to us by Williams, we waited listlessly for the day to end; none of us felt like

eating. It was hot and the room was stuffy, not helped by the small fire we had lit in a metal bucket to boil the water. It was too dangerous to remain outside even though it was cooler. The Creeps had become unpredictable, and there was always the slim chance that Kaminsky would send out some sort of patrol, though, personally, I thought it highly unlikely. Men like Kaminsky didn't think like that; their own perceived security made them arrogant, careless. It was one of the things I was counting on.

An hour before sunset, we gathered outside our refuge.

"Be safe," I said.

Tom and Nat nodded then headed east, intending to make their way to the other side of the Block.

Charlie and I went west, armed and hoping that the night wouldn't end in violence, but knowing if it came, we would be ready. I wanted to get into position while we still had daylight to reduce the risk of a surprise Creep attack. Noise precluded us from using the van; at a slow trot, we wound our way through the silent streets on foot.

Crouching by a low wall, I watched the roof of the Block. I tapped Charlie's shoulder and pointed as a single sentry sauntered into view, the beach umbrella I had taken up there slung over a guard's shoulder. We moved to the north corner of the building as he turned his back to us. Blue-black shadows pooled at the base of the building, stretching out across the road to our left as the sun descended. Darkness crawled into the sky, leeching the last of the day's light.

"I'm not sure if you're the canniest man I've ever met or the sneakiest," Charlie said as we stood beneath the carport of the house opposite.

"It was just a safety precaution," I said. "In case we ever had to evacuate as a last resort."

"You fixed the security mesh over the windows of your flat so they could be opened, even from the outside? At least that answers why you wanted to live on the first floor."

"It was too dangerous fixing the windows on the ground floor; it might have made tonight's job a little easier though."

"And only Jules and Trish know?" Charlie asked.

"For obvious reasons, if the Creeps ever got inside the Block, they were to get the kids to my flat and out the window," I said. "Come on, it's dark enough. Let's get this done."

Crossing the road, I retrieved a two-piece ladder from the garden of a neighbouring house. Charlie took the other end as we waited below my flat window.

"Sneakiest, I think," whispered Charlie.

The guard on the roof began shouting and was answered by someone down below in the courtyard. Booted feet thudded up the stairs.

"Looks like Tom's set the fires," muttered Charlie.

"Help me; we won't have a lot of time," I said, lifting the ladder.

Quickly ascending, I paused by my windows. Metal dustbins clashed in the night, glass smashed, the sound of wood pounding on cars filled the air.

"It's coming from over there."

"Is it the furballs?"

"Something's on fire, look! There and there!"

Twisting the fixing on the steel mesh, I pulled it free and swung it back against the wall. The window slid open silently, and I clambered inside. Moments later, Charlie followed. My bedroom was full of shadows with just enough ambient light to guide our way. The room was wrecked, the bed overturned, the wardrobe empty, my clothes strewn all over the floor.

"Kaminsky," whispered Charlie.

"Probably hoping to find more guns, or maybe just plain ol' fashioned spite," I said.

The hallway was well lit as I stopped by the bedroom door.

"The front door is open," I mouthed to Charlie. "Go for the kids. Protect them."

Keeping low, we slipped out onto the balcony, giving us a good view of the deserted courtyard. A shadow moved in the bus. I pointed at myself, then the bus, then indicated Charlie use the nearest stairs. He nodded his understanding. It seemed everyone was on the roof which was good. Only two oil drum fires were lit, making more shadows than giving light. Making my way round the balcony, I prayed not to be discovered. My mouth was dry; sweat stung my eyes and irritated my face. Swiping it away with a forearm,

I descended the stairs. The bus was to the right; the foot of the stairs clearly visible to anyone inside.

Hugging the wall, I kept my eyes on the shadowy figure who was more interested what was going on outside the arch than behind him. The door to the bus was open. I would have to move fast; as soon as I mounted the platform, he would know I was there.

The courtyard was alive with dancing shadows that made me jumpy. *How the hell am I going to silence the man without raising the alarm?* The roof had gone quiet; the bikers would soon get bored with nothing to see and descend. I had to do something. Holding position just below the windscreen, I felt the fear rising. *I have to move. I have to move now!*

"Hey! Who are you? What are you doing there?"

The shout was loud. I froze, wildly looking around to see who had discovered me.

"Hey!" shouted the voice again.

I heard the sounds of a struggle over by Jules' flat. *Charlie!*

I couldn't make out what was happening, just heard the grunts and shuffling of feet. Then gunfire blasted the night. I jumped again as the strobic effect of the muzzle flashes lit up the courtyard.

"Shit!" I cursed.

The hollow clumping of boots echoed from within the bus as a figure appeared in the doorway. Without thinking, I stepped out and drove the butt of my rifle into his stomach. The man gasped and doubled over as I clubbed him to the ground.

"They're inside the perimeter!" shouted a familiar voice. "Get back down there!" Kaminsky yelled.

Scrambling into the driver's seat, I started the bus, the engine roaring into life, drowning out the sounds of curses and running feet from above. A brief glance towards Jules' flat showed Charlie on one knee, his rifle trained on the stair well.

As I crunched the gears, the bus lurched forward, clearing the archway. Bullets ricocheted off walls and concrete steps as Charlie pinned the bikers on the stairs.

"Come on, you bastards! I'm ready for you!" he yelled, firing another short burst.

Charlie was oblivious to the stealthy figure creeping up from his right. A crossbow trained on him as he stood, clearly depicted in a halo of light from an overhead lamp.

"Charlie! Look out!"

Horror struck, I watched as the biker took aim, the deafening noise of gunfire drowning out my warning. Amazingly, the biker staggered, dropping the crossbow as an arrow pierced his shoulder. He stumbled over a box and fell headlong. He didn't get up.

Exiting the bus, I saw Nat dropping her bow and bringing up her rifle. She fired a fusillade at the stairs. Kaminsky's men ducked, hugging the concrete steps as stone chips flew all about them.

"Saved you again, Charlie Boy!" she called as she let loose another burst.

Charlie looked at her in surprise.

Seeing their descent blocked, the bikers turned tail and scrambled back up the stairs. Nat fired over their heads. They all ducked, hugging the stairs.

"Move and my next burst won't be so high!" Nat yelled.

I hurried over to Charlie.

"You okay?" I asked.

A body lay sprawled against a wall.

"Yeah, I didn't see him till I was right on top of him, scared the shit out of me. I think he was more surprised than me."

Kneeling by the body, I put my fingers to his throat.

"Is he dead?" Charlie asked shakily.

"No, took one in the shoulder. Looks like he cracked his head and knocked himself out, probably when he fell over the crate," I said, noting the blood in his scalp.

Charlie sighed heavily.

"Where are the others?" I said, getting up.

As if in answer, a frantic banging came from Nat's flat; men were shouting, demanding to be let out.

"Okay, okay, give us a minute!" I yelled. The clamour died down.

I wasn't surprised to find the security gate over the front door locked.

"Get away from the door!" I yelled.

Once sure they were out of harm's way, I shot out the lock, huffing when I discovered the deadbolt was engaged on the front door. I kicked it in.

Roger, Jules, and the Taylor boys came spilling out, full of relieved smiles and garbled questions, angry, but relieved.

"Where are the women?" I asked.

"In Charlie's place," said Jules. "They…"

"Best stand still, gents," grated a harsh voice. "I know reunions can be fun, but I think we can dispense with the weapons."

The Glock was in my hand and pointing straight at Kaminsky before it registered that he held Sally at knifepoint. Charlie and Nat raised their rifles. Kaminsky's smirk was cocky, arrogant. His knife glittered at Sally's throat. His fingers tangled in her hair as he pulled her around viciously.

"I don't think so, mate. We both know you're not good enough to make the shot without hitting the lovely Sally."

"It's over, Kaminsky. Let her go," I said evenly.

"Let me think about that for a second," he said, pouting his lower lip as if thinking. "Nah, I don't think I will."

"Shoot him, Adam. Shoot the prick! Shoot him!" urged Sally.

Kaminsky hauled on her hair again, and her face creased in pain as she whimpered.

"Will you be quiet? I'm trying to talk here," he said in Sally's ear.

"Bastard!" Charlie took a step forward.

"Uh, uh," Kaminsky warned.

"You've got nowhere to go," I said. "We've already got your men; you're on your own. If you hurt her, I promise you, you will pay dearly."

Kaminsky laughed. "Says you."

Tom Taylor was over by the chicken coop, slowly edging his way around to get behind Kaminsky.

"Just let her go and you can walk out of here," I continued. "No one will stop you or your men. Just leave."

"You keep talking as if you've got a say in this, mate. Let me enlighten you. You don't," Kaminsky said. "We got a good thing here: food, shelter, good company. Really good company."

I didn't like the way he said that or the sneer.

His face hardened. "Let my men go and lay down your weapons. Do it now. I'm losing patience."

Sally was trying to tell me something; her face was working, her eyes wide, but she wasn't afraid. I realised she was willing me to shoot, take the bastard down, but I couldn't. Kaminsky had been right on that score. I shook my head almost imperceptibly.

"Well fuck this," Sally said as she snapped her head back, catching Kaminsky on his very prominent nose and yanking down on his knife bearing hand at the same time.

Kaminsky grunted, staggered, but then reaffirmed his grip in her hair.

"Bitch!" he grated.

For a split second, he was off balance. Tom rushed forward, the butt of his rifle crashing into Kaminsky's temple. Sally twisted away as the big man went down. She cried out, clutching her neck, and then the knife skittered across the ground. With a roar, the biker tried to get up only to find himself staring down the barrel of Tom's rifle levelled at his head.

"Just give me an excuse," Tom said menacingly. "Please, just one."

Kaminsky sagged back down on the ground, his hand reaching for the gash on the side of his head. He grimaced when it came away bloody. He stuck his fingers in his mouth, licking them clean of blood and then contemptuously spat it on the ground, giving Tom a leering smile.

"You're welcome," Tom said wryly.

"Sally!"

She sat up, holding her neck. "The little shit cut me," she said.

"What the hell were you thinking?" I said, helping her up and checking the wound. Thankfully it was only a scratch. "You could have been badly hurt."

"Well, I knew you wouldn't shoot him, so I had to take matters into my own hands; no way was I going to let him get the better of me!"

I couldn't help but laugh. "You crazy cow." I hugged her.

People were milling about, relieved and glad to see their loved ones safe and unharmed.

"Put him with his friends," I said to Tom. "Make sure they're all tied."

"Adam," Sally said, suddenly serious. "He took Tina. On the first day, Kaminsky singled her out, and we haven't seen her since."

"Took her where?" I asked.

"Her place," Sally said.

"Stay here."

I headed for Tina's flat, Charlie and Julie in tow. The front door banged back against the wall as I hurriedly entered. The place stank of cigarettes and stale sweat.

"Tina! Tina, where are you?"

There was no reply.

I went into the living room while Charlie checked the bedroom.

"Adam! Here!" The urgency in Charlie's voice made me go cold.

Hurrying to the bedroom, I froze in the doorway. Tina's naked body was spread-eagled on the bed, tied by her hands and feet to the bedposts.

"Oh my God," I breathed.

Charlie was trying to untie the knots, but the rope was nylon and wouldn't give. Pulling out my knife, I cut her free, her wrists and ankles bloody and chafed. She moaned, pulling away from me, feebly slapping at my hands trying to hold her.

"Easy, easy, it's okay, Tina. It's okay..."

A rage welled up inside me as I looked at her bruised and battered face. Her left eye was completely swollen shut and her lips badly split, caked with blood. Tears stung at the back of my eyes as I held her close, trying not to see the cigarette burns on her breasts, her thighs, the lash marks standing livid across her back and buttocks.

"Oh, sweet Jesus..." Charlie said behind me.

There wasn't an inch of flesh that wasn't bruised, lacerated, or burned. She clung to me desperately, shoulders heaving as she silently wept.

"Get me a sheet or something," I said, my voice hitching in my throat. "We need to get her out of here."

Julie produced a clean sheet and helped me wrap it around Tina's shoulders. Leaning against me, her head down, Tina allowed me to lead from the flat.

The courtyard fell silent as we exited, audible gasps of horror escaped the shocked residents. They cleared a path as we headed for Charlie's flat.

Kaminsky's laugh was loathsome, mocking.

"She was sweet, Adam," he taunted. "Real sweet, but you already knew that, didn't you?" He laughed again. "Maybe we can compare notes?"

With me on her right and Charlie on her left, we guided Tina across the courtyard.

"She'll probably be able to teach you a few tricks now, mate," Kaminsky called. "She's a fast learner."

I felt Tina stiffen.

"It's okay; he can't hurt you anymore," I encouraged.

"Tell you what darlin', if ol' Adam there can't satisfy you now you've had better, you can always come find me..."

"For fuck's sake! Someone shut him up!" yelled Charlie.

Kaminsky laughed.

Through her tangled hair, Tina glared at him as he stood, his hands tied behind his back, a wide mocking grin on his thin lipless mouth. Her scream was sudden, shrill. She pushed me away with surprising strength; caught unaware, I staggered. Tina barged Charlie aside, his legs tangling in a chair, sending him sprawling.

Still screaming, Tina stalked towards Kaminsky. The sheet fell away from her tortured body; her terrible injuries seemed to glow in the ruddy light, sheened in sweat and blood.

"Knew you'd come back for..."

The gunshot blasted through the silence as people dived for cover; someone screamed. Kaminsky's men scattered. Kaminsky's colourless eyes popped open in surprise as the first bullet slammed into his chest, knocking him backwards. The second struck his left shoulder, spinning him round. The third missed. The fourth shattered his right shoulder blade, the fifth struck dead centre into his spine, and the sixth punched into his lower back.

Derek "Rambo" Kaminsky was dead before his face smashed into the unforgiving concrete, shattering his large nose and mashing his lipless mouth full of rotten teeth. Tina stood over his bullet-ridden body, still screaming, the empty gun clicking spasmodically in her shaking hands. I snatched up the sheet and threw it over her nakedness; my left hand slid down her arm and eased the gun out of her convulsing grip.

"It's okay," I said, holding her close. "It's okay."

Twenty-Five

December 2018

But it wasn't okay. None of it was okay. It was a massive cluster-fuck that left everyone reeling, me included. I couldn't think of that though; there was too much to do, too much to put right.

Julie and Sally took over the care of Tina, who had fallen into an almost catatonic silence. It worried me, but I knew she was in good hands.

"I didn't even feel her take my gun," said Charlie. "She was so fast."

"It wasn't anyone's fault, Charlie, so don't beat yourself up. The only one to blame was Kaminsky, and he paid the price," I said.

Several people had begun clearing up the debris littering the courtyard. Most of the flats occupied by Kaminsky and his cronies were a mess, and it was incredible how much mess in just two days. I saw Jules sitting by one of the fires, his head in his hands.

"Hey, Old Man," I said.

He raised his head.

"Ouch," I said, seeing his swollen cheek and cut lip.

"It's nothing," he said dismissively. "What a shambles," Jules added, sorrowfully looking around at his once happy home.

"No one could have known this would happen. I knew Kaminsky was a dick, but this..."

"He killed the chickens," Jules said. "Cooked 'em right in front of us, him and his cronies. Son of a bitch."

Looking around, the confusion and distress on the faces of all our friends was obvious and painful to see. Ironically, Kaminsky's men were being held in the chicken pen, poetic justice, maybe. We'd deal with them in the morning. I realised one of their number was missing.

"Where's Hogan?" I asked.

"I don't know," said Jules. "There was a fight when the other bikers turned up. Hogan wasn't happy with what Kaminsky was doing and tried to stop him. They beat the crap out of him. The last I saw, they dragged him off unconscious to his flat."

The door wasn't locked as Tom and I cautiously entered the flat. Like all the others, the place was wrecked. After a quick search, we found Hogan in the living room, out cold on the floor. It didn't look good.

"Let's get him into the bedroom," I said. "See if Sally's free."

Jules hurried off to get her.

"This is a nightmare," Charlie said as we sat by one of the newly lit fires in the courtyard.

I didn't have the words to answer.

"Julie finally got the kids settled. She's got Tina's twins as well; they kept asking about their mum. Thankfully they're all asleep now."

"What about all the other children?"

"They're shaken up, but Trish and Joan worked their magic. A few sweetie treats and a bedtime story sorted them out," said Nat.

It was not long past midnight, and no one was interested in sleeping. People sat in quiet groups about the courtyard, the air of defeat and despondency heavy in the air. Kaminsky's body was wrapped in plastic sheeting and put in a vacant flat out of sight. Jeff and Alan volunteered to get it out of the Block at first light. I didn't ask what they were going to do with it.

"We need to call a communal meeting early tomorrow morning," I said.

"Can't we give them a little time to recover from this lot?" asked Nat.

I could feel her sorrow, my heart was just as heavy, but what I had to say couldn't wait.

"Much as I'd like to, we can't," I said. "We're out of time. I don't know about anyone else, but I don't really want to stay here anymore. I'm tired of just reacting to situations as they arise; we need to be more proactive, make things happen the way we want them to, not just roll with the punches."

"The vines might have something to say about that," Charlie said.

"Which is why we need to act now," I said. "Jump before we're pushed."

"When you talk like that it usually means you got something crazy in mind," said Charlie.

I smiled bleakly because he was right. What I had in mind was crazy. It would sound even crazier when I said it out loud, but I couldn't think of any other plan of action.

I steeled myself.

"I haven't told you everything," I said. "Besides the vines and the Creeps, there is a much more imminent problem. I didn't say anything earlier because I wanted us to be all together. We all know about the Thamesmead situation, and we can't stay here. I don't believe Williams' assessment of the enclaves or the evacuation plans. Something's not right; I can feel it in my bones."

I briefly outlined what Williams had told me about Operation Inferno.

"But that's a good thing, isn't it?" asked Tom.

"No," I said, "these thermobaric devices are sometimes called aerosol bombs. They are designed to disperse a fine mist of explosive under extreme pressure, which is then ignited a split-second later. Something similar to napalm, only a hundred times more powerful. The result is a self-accelerating sheet of fire fuelled by the surrounding oxygen. The effect is devastating. Here's the pertinent point: there's no way to limit or control the blast."

The silence was complete.

"There's more," I said.

"Oh please," said Charlie.

"Even if the blasts are limited, the aftermath will leave massive fires; London will burn."

"But surely they know this?" said Jules. "They'll be fully aware of taking such measures."

"I believe the situation is out of control," I said darkly. "Whoever is in authority has decided that drastic measures are required, a 'final solution,' destroy London and everything in it."

"All the people at the camps?" asked Sally.

"I can't be sure," I said. "Maybe I'm wrong, but I believe that six days is not long enough to evacuate the populace. Regardless, we need to leave, and leave now. At the very least, we need to get clear of London within the next three days."

They all started talking at once. Jules finally calmed them down.

"We still have the same problem. Where do we go?" he asked.

"There was something Williams said about the Creeps that has been niggling at the back of my mind. He told me that the Creeps don't like the cold, which is why the weather's turned sub-tropical, another side effect of the black dust."

"And?" Jules asked.

"We can't fight the vines or the Creeps, so we need to go somewhere they can't go, somewhere cold," I said.

"Where?" asked Tom.

"Scotland," I said.

Epilogue

The morning was bright. A clear blue sky hung overhead, and the sun burned fiercely. It was a welcome sight after a very long night; it was good to finally see daylight again. Though I had been pressed after dropping the bombshell last night, I hadn't elaborated on my plans for Scotland. *How can I? I don't really have it sorted in my own head yet.* It just seemed the logical place to go, but getting there was another matter. That wasn't our top priority at the moment; getting as far away from the city as quickly as possible was. Real or not, we couldn't risk Operation Inferno.

The clearing up which started last night was only cursory. People were aware we were going to imminently leave. Though the air was one of reluctance, they had heard the news. Thamesmead was a bust, the Creeps were becoming more aggressive, and the vines were closing in. There was no other choice. We decided to keep Operation Inferno to ourselves; it served no purpose to create even more panic. Where we were going to go was on top of the speculation list. The evenings proposed meeting was highly anticipated. *I hope I'm not making a terrible mistake.*

Kaminsky's men were not welcome, but doing them harm was never an option. We gave them three days provisions, food and water, stripped them of their weapons, gave them a full tank of gas, and let them go with dire warnings; there would be no leniency should any of them return. Charlie's threats were particularly colourful.

Roger was looking at Kaminsky's Goldwing still parked in the corner, his hands thrust deep into the pockets of his corduroy trousers, his shoulders slumped.

"Hey Roger, looks like you got yourself a Goldwing after all!" said Charlie, slapping him on the shoulder.

Rodger's expression was grave, sad even. "I don't want it," he said distastefully. "Too many reminders, for Tina, as well as the rest of us."

Later that day, Roger took the bike and dumped it.

I was sitting quietly at the foot of the stairs, not really thinking of anything for once. I was just trying to enjoy a brief respite from the turmoil normally whirling about my brain. Watching Trish and the kids play catch across the way was good medicine. The laughter was infectious, a welcome tonic; the resilience of children never ceased to amaze me. Tom and his boys had gone out on a foray to get a few last things for the proposed journey north. Roger was tinkering with the van Charlie, Nat, and I had taken to Thamesmead. My ears were still ringing from the berating I got from him for the damage to the front offside wing. It was all good humoured; I think Roger was glad to have something to do. Very soon, after the meeting, supplies would be loaded into the vans, the bus would be armoured both sides, and everything we might possibly need would be taken for the journey north.

The sound of the motorbike had everyone reaching for loved ones. Trish gathered the children, herding them into the corner. Several guns were levelled at the open archway.

The biker cruised in slowly. The black leathers were worn, dusty, and the full-faced helmet obscured the rider's features.

"Hold it," I said as Charlie took aim.

The biker's hands were raised, showing they were empty. The bike stand was kicked down, and slowly dismounting, the biker stood silent.

"Who are you? What do you want?" I said, stepping forward.

The rider indicated the helmet, I nodded.

Making no sudden moves, the helmet was slowly removed, a gloved hand mussing the short brown hair clinging to a narrow head, soaked in sweat.

"What do I want?" she said easily. "You."

Stunned, I looked at her. The mocking brown eyes, the wide smile. She looked so different, yet there was no mistaking her.

"Linda...." I said.

ENDS.

Author Bio

Originally from London, United Kingdom, now settled in Texas, U.S.A, Alan Berkshire is a wanderer, writer, artist, and Pagan—a child who never grew up (and never will).

His two mainstays in life that keep him sane and supposedly grounded are his son, Nick, and his wife, Maria Elena. They make life worthwhile.

His other great loves are the outdoors, reading, movies, and superheroes.

Forever young.

More books from
4 Horsemen Publications

Fantasy, SciFi, & Paranormal Romance

Beau Lake
The Beast Beside Me
The Beast Within Me
Taming the Beast: Novella
The Beast After Me
Charming the Beast: Novella
The Beast Like Me
An Eye for Emeralds
Swimming in Sapphires
Pining for Pearls

D. Lambert
To Walk into the Sands
Rydan
Celebrant
Northlander
Esparan
King
Traitor
His Last Name

Danielle Orsino
Locked Out of Heaven
Thine Eyes of Mercy
From the Ashes
Kingdom Come

J.M. Paquette
Klauden's Ring
Solyn's Body
The Inbetween
Hannah's Heart
Call Me Forth
Invite Me In
Keep Me Close

Lyra R. Saenz
Prelude
Falsetto in the Woods: Novella
Ragtime Swing
Sonata
Song of the Sea
The Devil's Trill
Bercuese
To Heal a Songbird
Ghost March
Nocturne

T.S. Simons
Antipodes
The Liminal Space
Ouroboros
Caim
Sessrúmnir

Ty Carlson
The Bench
The Favorite

Valerie Willis
Cedric: The Demonic Knight
Romasanta: Father of Werewolves
The Oracle: Keeper of the Gaea's Gate
Artemis: Eye of Gaea
King Incubus: A New Reign

V.C. Willis
Prince's Priest
Priest's Assassin

Horror, Thriller, & Suspense

Amanda Byrd
sdfasd

Maria DeVivo
Witch of the Black Circle
Witch of the Red Thorn

Erika Lance
Jimmy
Illusions of Happiness
No Place for Happiness
I Hunt You

Mark Tarrant
The Death Riders
Howl of the Windigo
Guts and Garter Belts

Discover more at
4HorsemenPublications.com

CPSIA information can be obtained
at www.ICGtesting.com
Printed in the USA
BVHW041127080223
658123BV00015B/274/J

9 781644 506158